The Boy from Buzby Beach

A Buzby Beach Novel

DW Davis

7/24/18

D W Davis

The Boy from Buzby Beach

A Buzby Beach Novel / August 2014

This is a work of fiction. All names, characters, and incidents are the product of the author's imagination. Any resemblance to real persons, living or dead, is entirely coincidental.

Published by
River Sailor Literary
www.riversailorliterary.com

Originally published in eBook form by Master Koda Select Publishing in 2014

ISBN-10: 1545330026
ISBN 13: 978-1545330029

Cover Design © Rebbekah White
Wooden Walkway: sbgoodwin © Pond5.com
Boy and Girl on Beach © YayImages.com

Printed in the United States of America

D W Davis

ACKNOWLEDGMENTS

THE BOY FROM BUZBY BEACH introduces the Buzby Beach series to my readers.

THE BOY FROM BUZBY BEACH is a much smoother read thanks to my wonderful editor, Arlene O'Neil. The book's attractive cover is the work of my creative and artistic cover designer, Rebbekah White, who took my suggestions and changes in stride and turned my idea into a cover I love.

Added thanks go out to my lovely wife, Karen, and our sons – Alex and Zack – who have patiently (usually) and supportively acted as my proofreaders, sounding boards, and cheerleaders throughout the process from the first draft through the final edits. I could never have done this without them.

I would also like to acknowledge the contribution to the story in *THE BOY FROM BUZBY BEACH* of four of our family pets, three of whom are now departed, Jacques-our French Brittany whom we lost to cancer, Scout-our hurricane rescue mixed breed whom we lost to age, Ginger-my son's Brittany who is still entertaining us with her spunk and cuteness, and my cat, Joe, who is now prowling the fields beyond the Rainbow Bridge.

And finally, to all the folks who agreed to be Buzby Beach beta readers, thank you for helping me bring *THE BOY FROM BUZBY BEACH* to readers everywhere.

CONTENTS

CHAPTER ONE

A stiff sea breeze ruffled Jacques' shaggy black hair as he blinked the sleep out of his eyes and tried to focus on getting the key into the lock on the front door of his mother's coffee shop.

"Stupid lock," he muttered to himself. "Stupid street light. Why don't it light up the door better?"

So far, the first day of summer vacation wasn't much of one. His alarm went off at four in the morning so he could drag his butt out of bed and open the coffee shop for his mother. Since he'd turned fifteen two weeks before school let out, his mother decided Jacques could be responsible for opening the shop.

The Parisian Bean, referred to as The Bean by its regulars, opened for business at six in the morning, six days a week. Jacques' mom, Marie Babineaux O'Larrity, was usually in the cafe by five. The bakery that provided most of her pastries and bread dropped off every morning at five-thirty. Some specialty confections Marie baked herself. Jacques even baked a popular selection of spritz cookies. Marie let him keep the profit from those.

"Finally," Jacques said when the key slipped into the lock. He had to twist the key a little, jiggle the knob a couple of times, and twist the key the rest of the way before the door opened.

"I wish Mom would get this stupid lock fixed."

Jacques pushed the door open, pushed his glasses up his nose, breathed deep of the scent of roast coffee permeating the cafe, and stepped inside.

His hand absently searched for the light switch next to the door. The bright light coming from the chandelier that his mother had put over the sitting area caused him to squint against the glare.

"Ouch, that's bright. Stupid light."

Once his eyes adjusted to the light, Jacques turned, locked the door, and made sure the shade was pulled down. Then he rolled his eyes, pulled back the shade, and made sure the "CLOSED" sign was turned out toward the street.

"Stupid sign."

Growing up the son of a coffee shop proprietor, Jacques was never himself until he'd had his first cup of coffee. He didn't know for sure, but Jacques suspected his mother had filled his baby bottles with café latte.

Assured the "CLOSED" sign was indeed visible to any early risers, Jacques made a bee line for the espresso machine. With an expert touch born of years of experience, he'd been making espresso since he could reach the counter, Jacques made himself a Buzby Bucket sized caramel macchiato. The Parisian Bean was the only place in town where a person could get a 32 ounce cup of coffee. It wasn't cheap, but it was one of their best sellers during the summer tourist season.

"Mmm," Jacques moaned as the first warm, smooth, taste of the macchiato coated his throat and his body reacted to the promise of caffeine. As his mind reacted to the stimulant, the world didn't seem so stupid anymore.

Another long sip and he got down to the business of getting the cafe ready to open. He'd spent so much time helping Marie in the shop that getting it ready to open for the day was almost second nature to him. Joe Bagely, the delivery driver from the bakery, wasn't even surprised to see Jacques there at that hour filling in for his mom.

"Mornin' Jacques," Joe said in his easygoing drawl. "Your momma got you workin' bright and early this mornin'. I guess you're all done with school for the summer then?"

"Good morning, Mr. Bagley. Yes sir, today's the first day of break. Not much of a break for me is it, getting up at this time of the morning?"

Joe pulled off his Buzby Beach Bakery baseball hat and ran a pudgy hand over his balding head.

"I think it's right nice that you're opening the shop for your momma so's she can sleep late for a change."

Joe eyed the insulated carafe on the counter top where the donuts and muffins he'd brought would soon be displayed.

"I don't suppose you got any regular coffee brewed up yet this mornin', do ya, Jacques?"

Jacques smiled. "Just happened to start a pot brewing before you pulled up, Mr. Bagley."

He turned and took a cup off the stack.

"Let's see if I remember; you like yours with one shot of cream, and one spoonful of sugar, right?"

Joe nodded his head. "You remember right, Jacques. None of that fancy, foamy, la-tay stuff for me. While you get that, I'll bring in the rest of my delivery."

When Joe returned with the rest of the order, Jacques handed him his cup of coffee and started arranging the pastries in the display case. The Pari-Bean, as Jacques called it when his mother couldn't hear, had two large display cases. The one he was arranging with the goods from the Buzby Beach Bakery faced the front of the store and stood next to the counter where folks ordered their coffee. The other was set ninety-degrees to it, and behind it was a stainless steel table his mother used to decorate her cakes and cookies. These specialties, baked in house, were displayed in this second case.

The espresso and coffee machines were behind the main counter, separated by a single, stainless steel sink. To their right was a glass-door fridge for bottles of water and juice offered for sale. To their left was the door to the hallway leading to the back rooms and out the back door.

There were three back rooms. The first room was the kitchen where the ovens and stove were. Maria's hand decorated cakes, cupcakes, and cookies were in great demand on the island.

The second was the storage room. A closet in the storage room just big enough for a desk, chair, and lamp, served as an office. The last room was the bathroom. Paying customers were allowed to use the bathroom, upon request.

The front of the shop had several small tables, and a sort of bar opposite the specialty display case. Customers at the bar sat in stools, while customers at the tables sat in wrought iron chairs. Along the sidewalk in front of the shop, weather permitting, were a few tables with umbrellas and more wrought iron chairs.

Jacques finished arranging the display case about the time Joe finished his coffee.

"Can I get you another one of those, Mr. Bagley?"

Joe smiled, but shook his head.

"No thank ya, Jacques. I imagine I'd best be getting' on my way. What do I owe you for the java?"

"Compliments of the house, Mr. Bagley."

Jacques knew his mom never charged Mr. Bagley for his morning cup of coffee.

"That's mighty kind of you, Jacques. You tell your momma ole Joe said 'Hey,' you hear?"

"I'll tell her, Mr. Bagley. You have a great day, now. I'll see you bright and early tomorrow."

Joe stopped at the door and looked over his shoulder at Jacques.

"Maybe early, but I don't know how bright it'll be."

Jacques heard Joe laughing at his own joke as the door closed on him.

"Mr. Bagley is something else," Jacques muttered to himself.

Glancing at the clock, Jacques realized it was opening time. He made sure the insulated carafes of regular and de-caf were full, that fresh pots were brewing to replenish them, and made sure all the lights were on.

He'd raised the shades on the windows and doors, turned the sign around from "CLOSED" to "OPEN," and had no sooner gotten behind the counter when the door chime rang and in walked his first customer of the day.

"Good Morning, Mrs. Philbert," Jacques said.

He smiled as he recognized the co-owner of The News Stand. The News Stand, started by Mr. Philbert in the sixties, had morphed into more of a book store and gift shop, though customers could still find most of the big daily papers there.

"What can I get for you this morning?"

Mrs. Philbert set the stack of newspapers she'd brought in with her on the small oak table near the door reserved for such.

"I'll have my usual, and I'll need a Bucket for Herbert, just black. You know he doesn't like anything in his coffee."

The gray haired woman put her hands on her still shapely hips and frowned.

"I drink it black, the way God intended," Mrs. Philbert said in a fair imitation of her husband of forty some years.

Jacques chuckled. "Coming right up, Mrs. Philbert."

Mrs. Philbert's usual was a glazed donut and a cup of Parisian Blend, the house brew, with two shots of cream, two sugars, and a shot of hazelnut flavoring.

While Jacques prepared her coffee, Mrs. Philbert glanced towards the door to the back of the shop, and asked, "Where's Marie? Already in the back busy baking?"

Jacques set her coffees and donut on the counter. "No, ma'am. I got up early to open the store so my mom could sleep late."

Mrs. Philbert squinted one eye at Jacques and pondered the accuracy of that claim. She nodded slowly, deciding to give Jacques the benefit of the doubt.

"Well, that's a nice thing to do. You're a good son, Jacques. Your mother works hard: early mornings and long days. It's nice that you're getting old enough to be more of a help around here."

Jacques felt his cheeks redden at the compliment. "Yes, ma'am. I'm gonna be opening the store most days for the summer."

It wasn't exactly the way Jacques wanted to spend his summer. He'd rather sleep late, and then, when he did get up, spend the day on the beach and the night on the pier. He shrugged and shook his head before looking up at Mrs. Philbert.

"Is there anything else I can get you this morning?"

"Now that you mention it, my granddaughter is coming today. She's going to be staying with us a couple of weeks. You remember Cienna, don't you?" Mrs. Philbert asked, more to tease Jacques than because she doubted whether or not the boy remembered Cienna.

Jacques and Cienna had been nearly inseparable for the two weeks her granddaughter stayed each summer.

Jacques remembered Cienna. When she'd come to visit the Philberts the previous summer, Jacques was shocked to discover his summer friend had become an pretty young lady and he'd developed a huge crush on the petite fourteen year old with the jet black hair and dark brown eyes. Unfortunately for him, it was unrequited. Cienna only had eyes for Brennan, one of the life guards who usually manned the watch stand closest to the pier.

Cienna's crush on Brennan was even less successful than Jacques' crush on her. At least Jacques got to hang out with Cienna. Brennan barely noticed her. Ashlynn – South Hanover High's head cheerleader and homecoming queen - monopolized his attention.

Mrs. Philbert cleared her throat and smiled at Jacques.

"As I was saying, Cienna is coming today and I was thinking it might be nice if we had a cake made up for her. Maybe a 'Welcome Back to the Beach' cake."

Jacques walked over to the cake decorating table and grabbed a clipboard off its hook on the wall above the table.

"Let me make out an order for it, and I'm sure my mom will get right on it. What time is Cienna coming?"

Mrs. Philbert bit her lower lip and closed her eyes.

"Hmm, their flight gets into ILM at one. By the time they get their bags, pick up the rental car, and make it out of the airport, say it'll be close to two. Another twenty minutes or so here-" she opened her eyes and looked at Jacques, "- depending on the traffic on College Road, of course."

Jacques nodded.

Mrs. Philbert continued. "That puts them here around two-thirty. So I'll need the cake ready by two. Will that work?"

Jacques looked at the list of orders his mom had for the morning. There weren't many.

"I don't think that'll be a problem."

He added Cienna's cake to the list.

"What kind of cake do you think she'd like?" he asked, pencil poised.

"Oh, I think a regular yellow cake with that wonderful frosting your mother makes up will be just the thing. Bright colors for the edges and letters. I'll be back at two to pick it up."

Jacques smiled. "It'll be waiting for you."

He ran and held the door for Mrs. Philbert as her hands were full with the two coffee cups and the donut. While he was holding the door, his next customer arrived.

The girl who walked up to him and stood by the door had reddish-brown hair pulled back in a ponytail and a light sheen of sweat covering her face, arms, and legs. Jacques figured, based on the short running shorts and tank top she was wearing, that the girl had been for a run on the beach. She pulled the ear buds for her MP3 player out of her ears, turned her forest green eyes on Jacques and asked, "Are you open?"

Jacques, suddenly aware he'd been staring, blinked and shook his head. When the girl frowned he realized she thought the shop wasn't open yet.

"Yes, we're open. Come on in."

He pushed the door open and waved for her to go inside.

She tilted her head, gave him a puzzled grin, and walked in.

Jacques moved quickly around her and behind the counter.

"What can I get for you?"

The girl looked around the shop.

"Are you the only one working this morning? Where's Marie?"

Jacques looked hard at the girl.

"Marie's my mom. She'll be in soon. I opened up for her this morning. How do you know my mom?"

The girl closed her eyes and leaned her head, first to one side and then the other, stretching her neck. Watching her, Jacques' pupils widened, his heart started beating faster, and his breath caught in his throat.

When the girl opened her eyes and caught him staring at her again, she smiled.

He's kind of cute, in a nerdy kinda way.

"I've been coming in for a latte the last couple of mornings after my run. You must be Jacques. Marie told me she had a son my age."

Jacques nodded, an embarrassed grin on his face at being caught staring again. "That's me. I'm Jacques."

The girl giggled, and Jacques bristled. He knew he was awkward around pretty girls, but did she have to laugh at him?

The girl, noticing him tense up, said, "I'm sorry, Jacques. It's just that it was funny, the way you said you were Jacques right after I said you must be Jacques. I wasn't really laughing at you, just at the way it all came out."

Jacques took a deep breath. "It's okay. No big deal. So, you want a latte?"

His resigned tone pinched the girl's heart with a twinge of guilt.

"Hey, really, I didn't mean to hurt your feelings. Can we start over?"

She lowered her chin, smiled shyly, and looked at Jacques from under raised brows.

She looked so cute, gazing up at him through her long, delicate lashes, that Jacques couldn't stay irritated. Despite wanting to maintain his not-quite-a-scowl, he smiled. The girl took that as a good sign.

"Hi. My name is Ginger. My family just moved to the island. I hope we can be friends." She batted her lashes and curtsied.

The curtsy caught him so by surprise that Jacques laughed out loud. Since that was the reaction she was hoping for, Ginger laughed along with him.

"Does that mean we can be friends?"

Jacques caught his lips between his teeth to stifle his laughter. When he had it under control, he replied, "Yes, I think we can be friends. That'd be cool."

He was about to ask her where she'd moved from when the door chime sounded and a young couple walked in holding hands, smiling adoringly at each other.

Jacques said, "I'd better go ahead and make your latte."

The honeymooning couple was the first wave of the morning rush. Between steaming milk, brewing espresso, and filling bakery orders, Jacques felt like he was about to go down for the third time when his mother's familiar hairdo was spotted coming through the door. Marie weaved her way through the crowd, smiling and greeting customers, and soon made her way behind the counter to rescue her beleaguered offspring.

While Jacques continued to take and fill drink orders, Marie took over the bakery orders and cash register. As they settled into a rhythm, the tension that had been growing among the waiting customers dissipated, and smiles began to appear.

Marie often got smiles from male customers of The Parisian Bean. Her exotic good looks came from her French colonial grandfather, also named Jacques, and Vietnamese grandmother.

Marie's grandfather had been an important land owner in Vietnam before the Viet Minh ousted their French overlords. Monsieur Babineaux got out of the country, with his Vietnamese wife and nine year old son Gerard, and very little else, just ahead of Ho Chi Minh's forces. Finding his way back to Paris, Grandpa Babineaux went to work for an uncle in a coffee house along the Champs-Élysées.

Gerard eventually went to work in the coffee house, opened several more around France, and became quite a successful businessman. Along the road to success, he met and married Marie's mother, a student chef studying in Paris. Louise Sanders, of Hampstead, North Carolina, followed her dream of becoming a French Pastry Chef to Paris and never left.

So Marie, and through her, Jacques, came by their affinity for coffee and baking naturally. Unfortunately, Jacques never got to know his mother's parents. They only came to the States once to see him soon after he was born. Their flight back to Paris on July 17th left JFK and broke up over the ocean shortly thereafter.

Marie's parents never warmed up to her marriage to Sean O'Larrity. Considering Sean left when Jacques was three, and they hadn't heard from him since, Marie conceded they were probably right. But it didn't matter. She had Jacques and they had The Parisian Bean, and they were doing all right.

The morning rush dwindled to a trickle. Marie put a hand on Jacques' shoulder and gave it a squeeze.

"You did good this morning JQ," she said, using her nickname for Jacques. "Think you can handle it alone for a while so I can get started on some cakes."

Jacques' back straightened and his face brightened. "Sure, Mom. I got it."

Marie leaned over and kissed his cheek. Not for the first time, she noticed he'd grown taller than she was. Not that she was that tall at five-six. Still, she hoped he'd grow a few more inches.

Boys should be tall, she thought.

CHAPTER TWO

Jacques wet a towel and began mopping down the counter. He looked up when a shadow fell across its surface. He was surprised. He hadn't heard the door chime.

"Can I get a refill?" Ginger said, holding out her cup. Jacques straightened up, eyes wide.

"Have you been here the whole time?"

Ginger looked down at the counter and then up at Jacques' eyes.

His eyes are the color of a mocha latte, a gold-flecked mocha latte.

"I came in when that last guy went out," she said. "I waited by the cake case until you and Marie got done talking."

Jacques nodded. "That's why I didn't hear the door chime."

The sound of a mixer starting up made Jacques turn towards the back door.

"Sounds like my mom's getting started on her cakes."

He took Ginger's cup and began preparing her another latte. Ginger glanced up at the menu of coffees available.

"Oh, I almost forgot. I need a white chocolate mocha for my mom and a caramel macchiato for my dad."

"No problem. What size?"

Ginger raised her hand to her mouth and gnawed at her thumbnail. "I don't know. Larges, I guess."

Jacques picked up a 32 ounce Buzby Bucket cup. "This is our large." Ginger snorted.

"Really? People really buy coffees that big?" Jacques nodded.

"Believe it or don't. They do. I start every day with one."

"Wow." Ginger pointed to the 20 ounce cup. "I think that would be big enough." She looked at the cup her latte was in. It was 20 ounces.

"Hey, Jacques. How come you didn't ask me what size I wanted this morning?"

Jacques shrugged and said, "You don't look like a Buzby Bucket kind of girl."

Ginger's eyes flicked from right to left before focusing back on Jacques.

"Thanks, I think. But I bet I could drink a, what did you call it?" She looked at the menu. "- a Buzby Bucket sized latte."

"Really," Jacques said, his tone making it a challenge. "Then I'll fix you one tomorrow morning."

"It's a deal," Ginger said. "I'll show you."

Jacques put the cups in a carry-out tray and handed it to Ginger.

"Are your folks waiting out in the car?"

Ginger looked over her shoulder, and noticed an old blue Jeep Cherokee idling in front of the shop.

"That's not our car. My folks are next door."

Jacques cocked his head and gave her a puzzled look.

"Your parents are in an ice cream shop and sent you next door for coffee? Is the ice cream place even open?"

Ginger realized Jacques didn't know who her parents were.

"My folks are the ones who bought the old bar and turned it into an ice cream shop. Didn't your mother tell you? She's their landlord."

Jacques pursed his lips and his shoulders slumped.

"I knew someone had taken over the lease on the bar and was turning it into an ice cream shop. My mom told me that. And it would have been kind of hard not to notice all the work going on. I just didn't know it was your folks. I haven't seen you over there."

Ginger set the take-out tray on the counter and heaved a sigh.

"I've only been here once before, for like an hour, when Mom and Dad signed the lease." Jacques shook his head, still confused.

"But your folks have been here a couple of months getting the store ready to open. When are they going to open, by the way? They've already missed Memorial Day."

Ginger's face colored.

"I stayed home with my grandma so I could finish school at my old school, if you must know. Like it's any of your business. And if I'm lucky I'll go back at the end of summer, when school starts. I wanna graduate with my friends, not down here with a bunch of strangers."

Jacques backed away from the counter.

"Sorry I asked."

"Yeah, well," Ginger sputtered as she picked up the take-out tray again. "Anyway, I'll see ya."

As the door swung shut behind Ginger, Jacques took a deep breath and let it out slowly before taking a big pull from his Buzby Bucket.

"Guess I shoulda minded my own business."

"Minded your own business about what?" Marie asked him.

Jacques jumped, bumped into the counter, and almost dropped his macchiato.

"I asked that new girl, Ginger, when she thought her parents are going open their store and she got all bent out of shape."

Marie licked her lips and raised her eyes to the ceiling.

"They were hoping to be open last weekend for Memorial Day, but there was a hold up getting the permits. Some of the plumbing over there wasn't up to code and had to be replaced. By the way, since you own the building that cost you a small fortune."

Jacques's eyes narrowed. "Why do I have to pay for it? It was grandpa's building."

Marie shook her head and tried to hide a smile. "Don't sweat it, JQ. The repairs were paid for out of the rental account, just like they are for the other shops, or the apartments upstairs."

Besides the soon-to-open ice cream shop and The Parisian Bean, there were two other stores located on the building's first floor. On the other side of the coffee shop from the ice cream place was a T-shirt store, FitU2A-T, and at the end was a bicycle rental place, Buzby Beach Bikes. They also rented quadracycles and surreys.

On the second floor were three apartments, all facing the road, connected by a hallway along the back. The apartment Jacques and Marie lived in was a two bedroom that occupied the space over the coffee shop and T-shirt store. Each end unit was generously called a one bedroom apartment, but was more of an efficiency unit. The unit over the ice cream shop was vacant. The other one bedroom unit was occupied by a locally famous writer who spent a lot of time in the coffee shop.

Realizing he hadn't seen Mr. Warren in the shop that morning, Jacques asked Marie,

"Where's our resident author this morning? He didn't come in for his Irish Crème Cappuccino."

Marie had started decorating Cienna's cake. She stopped and looked thoughtfully at Jacques.

"I think Harry told me he'd be gone a couple of days visiting book stores up around Morehead City."

Jacques looked at the postcard rack near the cash register. The top slots held copies of Harry Warren's book, Beach Brats.

"Are those the last four copies we've got?" he asked, gesturing toward the rack.

"I think we've got more under the counter," Marie said. "Check and see."

Jacques bent over and looked under the counter.

"Yup. They're here."

"How many are under there?"

Jacques looked again. "Two."

Marie smiled. "Then Kelly must of sold two yesterday. Harry will be glad to hear that."

Jacques shrugged. He thought Beach Brats was a pretty good book, and Mr. Warren seemed like a nice guy, but sometimes when Mr. Warren got talking to his mom, Jacques got the idea that maybe the guy liked his mom. Worse, she might like him back.

Jacques didn't remember much about his dad. Sean left when Jacques was only three, but Marie and Sean were still married, technically. She'd never filed for divorce, and he'd never come back and asked for one. And she'd never dated, seriously anyway, that Jacques knew of.

"Do they sell many of Mr. Warren's books at The News Stand?" Jacques asked.

Marie didn't look up from the cake she was working on.

"I don't know. I guess so. You'd have to ask Mr. or Mrs. Philbert."

"Maybe I'll do that when they come to pick up the cake," Jacques said.

"Why don't you call them and tell them you'll take it over?" Marie said. "That way you'll get to see Cienna. The two of you have been friends forever."

The door chime sounded before Jacques had a chance to answer. A very tall, dark skinned gentleman in a suit and tie came through the door. He nearly had to duck to avoid hitting his head on the door frame.

Marie glanced at him over her shoulder, turned back to the decorating table, and then turned around and looked again. The gentleman touched his brow in a mock Scout salute. "Ma'am."

His voice had a deep timber that made Jacques think of a locomotive rolling by. The gentleman turned to Jacques and said, "Could I have your largest size plain black coffee?" Jacques held up a Buzby bucket.

"This is our largest size. It's 32 ounces."

"That'll do nicely," the customer said. "Tell me, son. How are the fish biting?"

Since Jacques spent more time at the pier playing video games than fishing, he had no idea how the fish were biting. Luckily, Marie kept up with such things, just in case customers should ask.

"The spot are always a good bet this time of year, and croaker. It may not be too late for blues, but the water is starting to get little warm for them," Marie said. "Come down to do some fishing, have you?"

"I was thinking of giving it a try, if I have time while I'm here. It depends on how long the sessions last at the conference." He reached up and rubbed his neck.

Jacques handed him his Buzby Bucket full of plain black coffee. Before taking it, the customer put his hands in the small of his back and stretched. Noticing Jacques's inquisitive look he said, "My rental car is a compact. I'd reserved an SUV. Can you believe a Cobalt was the only thing they had left at the airport?"

He paid for his Buzby Bucket, threw a dollar in the tip jar, nodded to Marie, and left.

When the door closed, Jacques turned to his mother. "What conference do you suppose he was talking about?"

Marie watched the man fold his tall frame into his compact rental car. "The only thing I know of is some accounting thing they have every year at the Coastal Tower Resort. He didn't look like an accountant, did he?"

Jacques shook his head. "He looked more like a linebacker."

With the accountant's departure, the shop was momentarily empty. Jacques took the opportunity to grab a broom and dustpan and clean up the customer area. Marie placed Cienna's finished cake into the display case and headed back to the kitchen to get the next one.

Just before nine, the door chimed and in walked Kelly, one of the shops two employees. Kelly was ostensibly the assistant manager. She worked Tuesday through Saturday from noon to four or so. The *or so* depended on whether there were customers who'd already been served finishing up their coffee and/or pastry. Sometimes *or so* stretched until four-thirty, at which time Kelly would start turning off the lights. If customers didn't take the hint, Kelly would suggest leaving them the keys so they could lock up, as she had to be on her way.

Most people took her hints good-naturedly. Once in a while a tourist would get grumpy. When that happened, Kelly would remind her - it was inevitably a her - that the shop closed at four and it was then well past four. For some reason Kelly, short, curvy, and blond, never got arguments from the male customers.

"Kelly is a professional student," Marie once told Jacques. "She's been going to UNCW for nearly ten years, and is working on her third master's degree."

When Jacques asked why, Marie replied, "She likes going to school. She takes a couple of classes each semester, makes enough working here at the shop to get by, and enjoys herself in the meantime."

Jacques had asked, "But why doesn't she use her education to get a job and be successful at something?"

Marie had gotten a faraway look in her eyes. When she refocused on Jacques, she said, "JQ, in her own way, Kelly is successful. She's happy with her life, and asks nothing more from the world than it let her live her life her way. Kelly's not hurting anyone, taking from anyone, and shares smiles and good humor with everyone."

She'd looked Jacques squarely in the eye. "I'd say she's been pretty successful, wouldn't you? At least by her definition of success."

Watching Kelly saunter into the shop, a smile on her face, practically glowing with positive energy, Jacques thought about what his mother said about the woman, and smiled.

"What's that smile for, JQ?" Kelly asked. "Is it because your favorite girlfriend just strolled in?"

Jacques shook his head. "I don't have a girlfriend, Kelly. You know that. I was just thinking how cool it is that you work here."

Kelly stopped, hands on hips, lips puckered, and regarded Jacques with an exaggerated frown. Then the smile returned her face.

She clapped her hands, and said, "Boy, you say the sweetest things sometimes. If you were a few years older, or I was a few years younger...."

"You'd still keep your hands off him because he's your boss' son," Marie said from the hall doorway.

"Absolutely, boss lady, ma'am. I'd absolutely keep my hands off him any time you were around."

Kelly squeezed past Marie and made her way down the hall to the closet they jokingly called the big office to sign in.

By the time she came out to the counter, the group of ladies informally known as the Nine O'Clock Club was taking seats around a pair of tables Jacques had pushed together in preparation for their morning tea and biscuit.

While the Nine O'Clock Club enjoyed their tea, biscuits, and information sharing - Jacques's mother insisted he not call it gossip - other customers came and went. One young man, whom Jacques recognized as the new Science teacher at the high school, spent quite a bit of time on his laptop, taking advantage of the free Wi-Fi

Jacques had recently convinced his mother to offer. When Jacques brought him a third raspberry mocha refill, he noticed the guy appeared to be doing work for an on-line class.

"Aren't you a student at South Hanover?" the young man asked.

"Yes, sir. I just finished my freshman year."

Jacques was pleased the man recognized him.

"I'm Fitz Finney. I took Mr. Gardner's place teaching Biology and Life Science. I don't think you were in any of my classes."

Jacques shook his head. "No, sir. I have Life Science in the fall. Maybe I'll be in your class then."

"Maybe," Mr. Finney said. He pointed to his laptop screen. "I get to spend my summer doing on-line courses for my masters. You spending yours working here?"

Jacques swept his arm in a gesture taking in the whole store.

"It's my mom's shop. I work for her."

"She's not looking for more help, is she?" Mr. Finney asked, a hopeful look on his face.

"No, sir. Between me, Kelly, and Cameron, we've got things pretty well covered."

The disappointed look on Mr. Finney's face made Jacques wish they needed the help. Then a thought hit him.

"You might try the ice cream shop next door. They're just opening. They might be hiring summer help."

Mr. Finney's expression brightened. "You think so?"

Jacques answered honestly. "I don't really know, but it's right next door. It's worth a shot asking."

Mr. Finney rubbed his chin. He took a deep breath and stood up.

"Can you keep an eye on my stuff for minute? I'll go over and ask. Can't hurt."

He took a step toward the door, stopped, and looked back at Jacques. "Kind of sad a teacher can't make enough to live off of without a part-time job, isn't it?"

Jacques didn't think it was that sad that a teacher needed a summer job to get by, but he didn't say so to Mr. Finney. Jacques's mom worked harder and longer hours than any teacher he knew. So did most of the business owners he'd grown up around. The only one who didn't was Mr. Snicket, the guy who'd owned the bar Ginger's folks were turning into an ice cream parlor. And he'd gone bankrupt at the end of last summer.

Mr. Finney was smiling when he came back.

"Well, they didn't say no. Mr. Mumples - that's really his name - said they hadn't thought about hiring help. Figured him, his wife, and his daughter could handle things. Then I asked him if they'd be able to keep up working all day seven days a week all summer. That's when he took my name and number and told me to come back by in a few days."

Mr. Finney went back to work on his on-line class. Jacques cleared the table vacated by the Nine O'Clock Club. They'd each left a dollar on the table. He stuck the four bills in Kelly's jar. Kelly always took care of the Nine O'Clock Club ladies herself.

Kelly grabbed him from behind just as he straightened up from putting her jar back under the counter.

"Caught ya red handed!"

She laughed at the way Jacques jumped.

Jacques turned on her, his face red with embarrassment.

"You scared the sh-" he stopped mid-word when he saw his mother watching him over Kelly's shoulder. "-out of me." He pressed his lips into a thin line and stomped past his tormentor.

Kelly shrugged apologetically. "I was just having some fun."

Marie shook her head. "He'll get over it."

Jacques called out from down the hall, "No I won't. She's scarred me for life."

Marie and Kelly rolled their eyes at each other and laughed.

"He's over it," they echoed.

Things were slow but steady for the rest of the morning. Customers came and went, mostly to-go orders. A few occupied a table or a seat at the bar for a cup or two. Now and then, someone would come in to order one of Marie's decorated cakes.

CHAPTER THREE

Noon rolled around and the shop's other employee, Cameron, strolled in.

Cameron said, "Good Morning Jacques, and to you too, Kelly," with an accent that Jacques found pleasing and intriguing. It had British undertones, but carried distinct nuances of her Kenyan home.

"Have we been very busy today?"

Jacques smiled. Cameron always came in and asked the same question.

"It's been steady," he said. "My mom's been busy with lots of cake orders."

"Steady is good," Cameron said. "I shall be prepared for a steady afternoon, then."

Cameron took her station behind the counter. Jacques looked at Kelly, his eyes and the set of his mouth asking the question.

Kelly curled her lip and nodded her head.

"Yes, Jacques, you can go, but check with your mom first."

Jacques ran back to the kitchen.

"Hey, Mom. Cameron's here and Kelly says I can go. You need me to do anything before I take off?"

Marie set the sheet pan she'd just pulled from the oven on the counter to cool.

"Why don't you take Mrs. Philbert's cake over to her? And what are your plans for lunch?"

"I thought I'd hit Iggie's for a burger. He was supposed to install a milk shake machine this week. I wanna try it out."

Marie walked over, put her arms around him, and gave him a quick hug. "If you ride your bike, just be careful. Summer traffic, you know."

Jacques shifted restlessly from one foot to the other.

"I know, Mom. I'll be careful."

Marie lowered her chin and looked up at Jacques with serious eyes.

"And walk Mrs. Philbert's cake across the street before you go see Tony and get your bike, you hear me?"

"Yes, Mom. I will."

He started for the door, but Marie wasn't finished.

"And why don't you see if Ginger from next door wants to go?"

Jacques stopped cold.

"I don't think she'd want to go with me. She's probably not there anyway. I bet she went home."

Marie fixed him with a don't-give-me-that stare.

"It won't take you a minute to stop next door and see."

Jacques' shoulders slumped. "Yes, ma'am. I'll see." Then a mischievous gleam came to his eyes. "Can I go now?"

Marie put her left hand on her hip, wagged her right index finger at Jacques, and said with exaggerated slowness, "May I please go now?"

Jacques eyes widened in mock horror. "You want to come, too?"

Marie huffed dramatically and narrowed her eyes.

Jacques laughed.

"Okay, Mom," he said. Folding his hands under his chin, his voice all sugar and spice, Jacques asked, "May I please go now?"

Marie reached up and ruffled his hair. Laughing and shaking her head, she said, "Yes, you brat. You may go now."

As he darted out the door, Marie called after him, "I love you, JQ."

She barely heard his, "Love you too, Mom," as he rounded the end of the counter and headed out the front door.

Jacques stopped at the front door, a sheepish grin on his face. He turned to the cake case and there stood Kelly, holding Mrs. Philbert's cake.

"Did you forget something?" she asked him, raising one eyebrow.

"I didn't forget. I almost forgot," Jacques said, stepping over to the case and taking the cake from Kelly's hands. "Almost forgot doesn't count."

Outside on the walk, Jacques gnawed at his lower lip, trying to decide if he should do as Marie suggested and ask Ginger to go with him to Iggie's. He looked across the street at The News Stand, next door at The Sand Bar - only now a sign that looked like a waffle cone topped with vanilla ice cream hung where the old Sand Bar sign used to be - and then towards the other end of the building at Buzby Beach Bikes, where Mr. Bishop, the owner, let him keep his Schwinn Corvette Deluxe Beach Cruiser.

The Beach Cruiser had been Jacques' Christmas gift from Marie two years before. It was a quality bike and Marie made it clear when she gave it to him that how well he took care of it would weigh heavily in her decision as to whether he could have a car when he turned sixteen. Keeping that in mind, Jacques took very good care of his bike.

Deciding to deliver the cake first, then ask Ginger, and then get his bike, Jacques looked both ways before crossing the street to The News Stand. He took his mother's warning about summer traffic to heart.

When Jacques was eight he saw a patron, who'd had one too many, leave The Sand Bar and walk right out in front of an inlander - the residents' name for anyone who wasn't a resident of the island - who was busy admiring the shops along Sound Street. The image of the man being knocked to the street always popped into Jacques' mind just before he stepped off the sidewalk.

Fortunately, the inlander had been moving at a crawl and the inebriated jaywalker escaped with nothing but scrapes, bruises, and soiled britches.

The pair of silver bells over the door jangled when Jacques entered The News Stand. Mr. Philbert looked up from the paper he was reading at the checkout counter and smiled. "What ya got there, JQ? Is that Cienna's cake?"

Jacques set the cake down on the counter. "Yes, sir. I hope she likes it."

Mr. Philbert scrutinized the cake before replying. "It looks real nice. Your mother does good work, Jacques. Are you gonna be here to help us welcome Cienna back?"

"Yeah, I think so," Jacques said.

Then he noticed the disapproving look Mr. Philbert was giving him. Herb Philbert was the closest thing Jacques, who'd never gotten to know any of his grandparents, had to a grandfather.

"I mean, yes sir. I'll be here."

"That's better," Mr. Philbert said, his expression softening. "I know Cienna is looking forward to seeing you again."

Mr. Philbert took the ticket off the cake box. "I'll give this to Beverly. She'll drop a check off in the morning when she comes by for her daily dose. So what are you up to now, young man?"

"I'm headed over to Iggie's to try out his new milkshake machine. It's supposed to make shakes just like the ones you get at Mickie D's."

Jacques licked his lips at the thought. It might annoy Marie, but Jacques loved a McDonald's chocolate shake.

While Marie tolerated Jacques eating at Iggie's - Iggie was a neighbor and a friend - she wasn't a fan of fast-food places.

"I heard Iggie bought one of those machines. Wonder what made him decide to do that after all these years?"

Mr. Philbert rattled his newspaper and went back to reading.

Jacques realized Mr. Philbert wasn't expecting an answer.

"I'll see you later, Mr. Philbert."

"See ya, JQ," Mr. Philbert replied from behind the business section.

The silver bells jangled again as Jacques left The News Stand. He stood on the walk, looking back and forth from The Beach Cone to Buzby Beach Bikes. With a resigned sigh, after checking both ways, he crossed the street and walked in the open door of the ice cream parlor.

A tall man with a paint roller in his hand, whom Jacques recognized as Mr. Mumples said, "I'm sorry, but we're not open yet," when Jacques walked in the door.

"Yes, sir. I know. I'm Jacques from next door."

Jacques pushed his glasses up his nose and ran his hand over his hair.

"I was wondering if Ginger was here."

Mr. Mumples carefully set the paint roller into the tray at his feet, stretched his back, and gave Jacques an appraising look.

"I didn't know you'd met my daughter."

Jacques' barely protruding Adam's apple bobbed as he swallowed. He licked his lips and said, "We met this morning when she came over to get some coffee. I was just wondering if she'd like to go with me to Iggie's."

Mr. Mumples rubbed his neck and stretched his head from side to side.

"Iggie's? That burger place down near the beach? I haven't tried it yet. Is it any good?" Jacques nodded vigorously.

"I love Iggie's onion rings. And he's got a new milkshake machine."

Mr. Mumples bent forward and put his hands on his knees, rolling his shoulders forward as he did so. Jacques figured the man must be worn out from all the work he'd been doing getting the store ready to open.

"I guess it would be all right. Are you going to walk?"

Jacques hadn't thought about that. *What if Ginger doesn't have a bike? She probably doesn't have a bike. Maybe Mr. Bishop will loan her one.*

"I was gonna ride my bike," Jacques said. "But I can walk if Ginger doesn't have a bike." Mr. Mumples pressed his lips together and looked toward the back of the shop.

"Ginger, have you got your bike here?" he called out.

From somewhere in the rear of the store, Ginger called back. "What do you need my bike for?"

Mr. Mumples shook his head.

"I don't need it, but you might. Could you come out here, please?"

Ginger appeared from a room along a hallway that mirrored the one in the back of The Parisian Bean. Jacques guessed it was probably a storage room when the place was The Sand Bar.

She stopped short when she saw Jacques standing next to her father.

"Hi. What are you doing here?"

Jacques started to tell her, but Mr. Mumples said, before he could, "Jack here wants to know if you want to go to lunch at Iggie's. If you have your bike, you two can ride there. If not, I guess you'll have to walk."

Ginger rolled her eyes at her father.

"His names Jacques, Dad, not Jack. Jacques. And no, my bike's at the house. But I think the house is on the way to Iggie's."

She turned to Jacques. "Could you walk your bike to my house and ride from there?"

"Uh, yeah, sure. I could do that," he said. "So you want to go?"

"Anything to get out of here for a while," Ginger said, looking at her red, wrinkled hands. "I've been scrubbing all morning."

"What are you complaining about?" Mr. Mumples asked, an edge to his voice. "I've been working my butt off trying to get this place ready for months."

Ginger hung her head. "I know, Dad. I'm sorry. I didn't mean nothing. But it is lunchtime. Can I go? I'll bring you back a burger or something."

Mr. Mumples sighed and put a reassuring hand on Ginger's shoulder.

"I'm sorry, too. I shouldn't have snapped at you. Yes, you can go. Bring me back a bacon cheeseburger, all the way. You know how I like 'em."

Ginger gave her dad a hug. Mr. Mumples bent down and picked up the paint roller and before they could go out the door, he was already applying one last coat of white paint to the interior wall of the seating area.

Ginger pointed her thumb over her shoulder.

"I don't know where he got the idea from, but opening up an ice cream shop down here at the beach has been his dream for years. He told me he used to come down here with my grandma and grandpa for a week every summer and every night they'd go for ice cream. He's told me that story a thousand times."

"I know my mom's glad your dad's turning the place into something besides a bar," Jacques said, glancing in the window of The Parisian Bean as they passed by.

Mr. Finney was still sitting at the bar working on his laptop. Cameron was setting yet another cup of coffee down for him. Mr. Finney looked up and smiled at her. The smile she gave him back looked like more than just the friendly smile she gave most customers. Jacques shook his head. *I'm imagining things.*

Ginger nudged him with her elbow. "Did you hear what I said?"

Jacques hadn't.

"I asked you why your mom didn't like the bar," Ginger said.

"Mostly the noise," Jacques said. "Especially on the weekends. They stayed open 'til all hours and Mom has to get up early to open the coffee shop."

As they walked by the entrance to FitU2A-T, Mr. Lemon waved them to a stop.

"Hey, JQ. Who's your friend?"

Jacques smiled at Mr. Lemon. The tall, fit, shopkeeper was the spitting image of his famous uncle, whose poster adorned a place of honor behind the counter in FitU2A-T. Jacques had met the Clown Prince of Basketball once, when he'd visited his nephew at the store during a visit to Wilmington for the unveiling of his star on Wilmington's Walk of Fame.

"This is Ginger Mumples, Mr. Lemon. Her dad is fixing up The Sand Bar as an ice cream shop. Ginger, this is Mr. Lemon. He owns the t-shirt store. He's got some really cool t-shirts."

"I've met your daddy, young lady. Seems like a fine man," Mr. Lemon said, taking her outstretched hand. "I hope things work out for you here."

"Thank you, sir," Ginger said, tilting her head back to meet Mr. Lemon's eyes. "I'll have to stop by and check out your shirts."

"You do that," Mr. Lemon said. "I'm sure I've got somethin' in here that you'll like."

To Jacques, he said, "Your momma's been busy baking today, JQ. How about you? When are you going to bake some more of your famous cookies?"

Ginger coughed. Jacques turned to her, his eyes wide.

"You bake?" she asked, unable to suppress a smile.

"Yeah, so. What's wrong with that?"

Ginger took a step back.

"Nothing. Boys can bake. I think it's cool that you bake. It just surprised me, that's all."

Mr. Lemon patted Jacques on the back. "Jacques here bakes the best little sugar cookies I've ever had. They're real popular on the island around the holidays, the way he decorates them up. He can hardly keep up with the orders."

Ginger's expression changed from incredulous to impressed.

"You bake, like, professionally? People buy your cookies? That's so cool."

At Buzby Beach Bikes, Mr. Bishop wasn't there, but his son Tony offered to let Ginger borrow a beach cruiser.

"Just drop it off when you come back," Tony said, smoothing down the front of his dark gray muscle shirt. "First day's rental is on the house for our new neighbor."

Jacques didn't like the way Tony was looking at Ginger.

"She's got a bike. We're gonna stop at her house and pick it up on the way." Ginger smiled shyly at Tony and brushed her hair over her ear.

"I think I'll try a beach cruiser. I don't know if my 12-speed could handle the sand."

Tony seemed all too happy to help Ginger pick out one of the rentals and make sure it was adjusted just so.

Tony had just finished his first year at Cape Fear Community College. His dreams of playing college football had come to a crushing end in the second to last game his senior year when he tore his ACL taking a hard hit as he tried to run the ball into the end zone. To add insult to injury, he'd fumbled the ball and the Buccaneer linebacker who'd picked it up ran it all the way back down the field for a touchdown.

Jacques rolled his bike to the curb and looked over his shoulder at Ginger and Tony. "We should probably be getting going."

Ginger looked at Tony, sighed, and shrugged. "I guess I've got to get going. I'll see you when I bring the bike back?"

Tony touched her lightly on the arm. "You can count on it."

Jacques pushed down on his pedals and bumped over the curve into the street. A car horn sounded, and he snapped his head around to see a Jeep Wrangler full of college age girls braking hard to avoid hitting him.

"Why don't ya watch where you're going?" the dark haired driver called out, lifting her Ray Bans from her eyes to scowl at him.

Jacques muttered a curse under his breath and pulled his bike up next to the curb. The girls in the Jeep laughed as they drove by.

Ginger wheeled her bike up next to him. "That was a close one."

Jacques, his face red, glared after the Jeep. "Stupid girl oughta watch where she's going."

"Well, you did pull right out in front of her," Ginger said. "She was paying enough attention not to run you over."

The hurt of her betrayal showed in his eyes when he turned from glaring at the Jeep to look at Ginger.

"Yeah, whatever. Are you coming, or do you want to stay and talk bikes with Tony?"

Now it was Ginger's turn to glare. "What is your problem?"

"I don't have a problem," Jacques said. He shoved away from the curb and pedaled off.

"Keep up, if you can."

Ginger didn't have any trouble keeping up with Jacques, even on an unfamiliar bike. She'd competed in her first junior mini-marathon earlier in the spring, back in Sanford, the town she still thought of as home. But she didn't go flying by him like she could have. First off, she didn't know how to get to Iggie's. In the second place, Jacques was the first kid her own age she'd met in Buzby Beach. He seemed like a nice guy, and since her dad's store was right next to his mom's, she figured they'd have to see a lot of each other. That'd be easier if they were friends.

Jacques looked back over his shoulder to see if Ginger was following. His heart gave a little flutter when he saw her keeping pace with him, just a few bike lengths back. After flashing her a quick smile, Jacques braked to a stop at the end of Third Street. Traffic on Ocean Street wasn't too bad, and he would've had no problem making the turn without waiting, but he decided to let Ginger catch up.

"How do you like the bike?" he asked when she stopped next to him.

She tilted the beach cruiser back and forth between her legs and shrugged.

"It rides nice, but I wouldn't have picked this color."

Mr. Bishop's rental bikes were either neon orange or neon green. They were not colors available on bikes you'd buy at your local Dick's Sporting Goods.

Jacques laughed. "I know what you mean. Mr. Bishop says it helps keep people from wanting to keep them. Steal them, he means. You can tell from a mile away it's a Buzby Beach Bikes bike."

Ginger saw an opportunity to smooth things over with Jacques.

"I like the color of your bike. Kind of a silver gray, isn't it? With metal flakes. I love the red rims."

Jacques felt a warmth spread from his chest, up his neck, to his face. *Oh God, I hope I'm not blushing.*

"Really? I wasn't too sure about the red rims when I first got it, but I think they look good with the gray frame."

Ginger nodded, her smile genuine. "They do. It's a good look."

When the next break in traffic opened up they turned left onto Ocean Street and half-a-block later made a right into the parking lot next to Iggie's. The burger joint was busy, with lines at both order windows.

"Looks like we'll have to wait in line," Jacques said as he wedged his front tire into the bike rack. "But don't worry, it'll be worth it."

Ginger looked up at the sign on the roof over the order windows and laughed. In small print under the "IGGIE'S BURGERS AND RINGS" was printed, "These are the burgers Jimmy sang about."

Jacques, wondering what she was laughing at, followed her gaze.

"Do you know that Jimmy Buffet song?" Jacques asked.

Ginger gestured at the sign, and said, "Well, yeah. Who hasn't heard 'Cheeseburger in Paradise'?"

"So, are you a parrot-head?" he asked.

"I'm not. Not really," Ginger replied. "But my mom is a major Jimmy Buffet fan. She's been to a ton of his concerts."

"My mom's a big fan of his too," Jacques said.

They were almost to the window when a familiar looking pink Jeep Wrangler pulled into the lot.

"Well," called out the driver from behind her Ray Bans, "look who's here. It's Evil Bo-weevil, the Rebel Daredevil."

The girls sitting in the back laughed. The girl in the passenger seat shook her head slowly, looked at Jacques, and mouthed, "I'm sorry. She's a jerk."

Jacques felt his temper rise as the dark haired driver teased him, but after seeing the other girl's reaction, curiosity cooled his ire. He hadn't noticed when the Jeep had been bearing down on him, but the girl in the passenger seat seemed younger than the other girls. Maybe more his age. Her dark brown hair hung loose around her face, hiding her features.

Jacques' scrutiny must have made the girl uncomfortable, because she looked away, lowered her chin, and aimed her eyes at the floor of the Jeep.

Ginger meanwhile, bristled at the way the older girl picked on Jacques. In response, she moved closer to her new friend and hooked her arm around his. Looking up at the menu she said, "What do you think I should get,

JQ? I haven't been here before. Why don't you order for me?"

She turned and shot a withering look at the Jeep's driver. The older girl put on a disinterested expression and turned to her friends.

Before Ginger turned back to look at the menu, she noticed the younger girl, who was still sitting in the Jeep, watching her with a sad frown forming on her face.

Ginger thought about the disappointment on the girl's face at the sight of her linking arms with Jacques. Then Ginger moved so her mouth would be close to Jacques' ear.

"I think you have an admirer."

Jacques' heart jumped when Ginger put her arm around his, and again when Ginger called him JQ and told him to order for her. It leaped a third time when she whispered he had an admirer. Jacques logically concluded she meant herself.

But when Jacques looked into Ginger's eyes, Ginger gestured with a nod of her head toward the pink Jeep and the girl still sitting in the passenger seat. Jacques turned his head and noticed the girl was watching the two of them. His lips twitched up in an uncertain smile. He turned to Ginger and licked his lips.

"Her, I thought you meant...."

Catching his meaning, Ginger's eyes grew big. "You thought I meant me. No, I...."

CHAPTER FOUR

"Hey Scar," the dark haired girl who drove the pink Jeep hollered at the girl still sitting in the passenger seat. "You gonna come get some lunch? I'm not gonna bring it to ya."

As Jacques watched, the girl named Scar swung her legs out of the Jeep and slid slowly from the seat until her feet touched the ground. After pushing herself upright, she turned and said to the Jeep driver, "You're such a j-jerk, K-kaitlynn. I was c-coming."

Kaitlynn tossed her head, letting her feathered black hair settle behind her shoulder before replying.

"Well little sister, you were taking your sweet time."

One of the girls from the back seat shoved Kaitlynn's shoulder.

"Hey, go easy on the kid."

"Butt out, Trish. I'm not gonna baby her," Kaitlynn said. "If she wants to tag along, she's got to keep up." She turned to her sister. "Come on, Scarlett. We don't have all day."

While this exchange was taking place, Scarlett was making her way from the Jeep to a spot in line next to her sister. Jacques couldn't tear his eyes away. He never noticed Ginger dropping her arm from around his.

Scarlett walked with the stiff gait of a person decades her elder. When she got closer, Jacques could see a scar running from above her right eye toward the bridge of her nose. Her nose looked like it had been mashed, and then reshaped by someone who wasn't quite sure how it had looked before being smashed. The scar reappeared just below her left nostril, crossed her lip, and disappeared below her chin.

Jacques noticed all this, but it wasn't the scar or the misshapen nose that held his attention. It was Scarlett's wide, round, beautiful gray-green eyes that captivated him.

Scarlett noticed Jacques staring at her. Heat started to color her cheeks, and she snapped at him.

"What are y-you looking at?"

Jacques shook his head as if he'd been slapped. Caught off guard, he answered honestly.

"You have really pretty eyes."

Whatever retort Scarlett had ready on her lips went unsaid. She closed her mouth and swallowed hard.

"Y-you really think so?"

"I do," Jacques said. "They're beautiful."

Beside him, Ginger stared at Jacques, disbelief on her face. Only a moment ago he'd been disappointed Ginger wasn't his admirer, and now he was ignoring her completely. She wasn't sure how she felt about that.

Kaitlynn started to say something to Jacques about staring at Scarlett, but Trish shushed her.

"He's not being rude," Trish whispered. "I think he likes her."

Scarlett took a shuffling step towards Jacques. She could only smile with half her face, but the half that could smile was lit up. Jacques took a step towards her, before he remembered Ginger there at his side. He stopped and looked from Scarlett to Ginger and back. Ginger put a hand on his back and nudged him towards Scarlett.

"Uh, hi," Jacques stammered. "I'm Jacques O'Larrity. My friends call me JQ."

"Jacques O'Larrity. Really?" Kaitlynn said with a laugh.

Scarlett sent her a look that would have melted most people. Kaitlynn didn't melt, but she did stifle her laughter.

Scarlett said, "Y-you'll have t-to ignore my sister. Y-you've p-probably noticed she's a real j-jerk some t-times."

Kaitlynn started to say something, but Trish slapped her in the back of the head.

"Hey, cousin or no cousin, you've gotta stop doing that," Kaitlynn said.

"I'll stop smacking you when you stop being a jerk," Trish said.

Kaitlynn turned to the fourth girl from the Jeep. "Marissa, can you believe them?"

Marissa nodded her head.

"You kind of had it coming, Kaitie-did."

Kaitlynn shook her head.

"I can't believe you guys, ganging up on me."

Then she did the last thing either Jacques or Ginger expected. She started laughing.

"Well, it looks like the votes three to one against me."

With a look at Jacques and Ginger, she amended her count.

"Make that five to one against, I guess."

Kaitlynn took a deep breath, closed her eyes, and they could almost hear her counting silently to five.

"Okay, kid. I'm sorry I almost ran you over." This was addressed to Jacques. "But you did ride right out into the street."

"Scar," Kaitlynn said to her sister, "I'm sorry I got on your case about taking your time getting out of the Jeep. It's just...well, you know."

From the look on Scarlett's face, Jacques guessed that this sudden change in Kaitlynn wasn't unusual. He wondered if she might be bipolar or something.

Further exchanges of not-so-pleasantries were forestalled by Iggie.

"Hey, if y'all aren't gonna order nothing, get out of line, will ya? Hungry people are waiting."

Jacques turned towards the window. "Sorry, Iggie. Um, I'll have a bacon cheeseburger, lettuce only, with onion rings and a chocolate milkshake."

Iggie wrote down the order on his pad, shaking his head.

"Ain't got chocolate. Only vanilla today. New machine only makes one flavor at a time."

"Okay, vanilla then." Jacques turned to Ginger. "Do you want me to order for you?"

"Not really," Ginger said. To Iggie she said, "I need two bacon cheeseburgers, all the way, two orders of onion rings, and a diet Coke."

Iggie looked at Scarlett. If he noticed her scars, he didn't show it.

"Are you with JQ, too?"

Scarlett's brow furrowed as she gave Iggie a puzzled look.

"What, who?"

"JQ is me," Jacques told her. "It's kind of my nickname. My mom started it."

"She's with me," Jacques said to Iggie. "Put her lunch on my tab."

Jacques turned to Scarlett. "That's okay, ain't it?"

"I g-guess so," Scarlett said. "If your g-girlfriend d-doesn't m-mind."

Jacques cocked his head. "My girlfriend? Oh, you mean Ginger?"

Before Jacques could say it, Ginger told Scarlett, "Jacques is not my boyfriend. We're just good friends."

Since Jacques had been about to say those same words himself, he was surprised how much it stung to hear them from Ginger. Sure, they'd only known each other a few hours, but he'd hoped somewhere in the back of his mind, that Ginger might be the one to end his girlfriend drought.

"Oh," Scarlett said, her smile returning. "In that case, I think I'll have a ch-chicken b-burger with lettuce and t-tomato, French fries, and a d-diet Coke."

"Are you sure you don't want to try Iggie's onion rings?" Jacques asked. "They're the best anywhere."

Scarlett shook her head. "I'm not b-big on onions."

Seeing the disappointment in Jacques' eyes she added, "Maybe I'll t-try one of yours."

"Scar," Kaitlynn said. "If you're done ordering, step aside. We need to get our food and get moving on down to the beach."

Scarlett moved aside. "We're not g-going to eat here?"

"Uh, no," Kaitlynn said. "We'll eat in the Jeep after we find a good parking spot near the beach."

"Oh," Scarlett said. She turned to Jacques. "I g-guess I'll t-try the onion rings s-some other t-time."

"Sure," Jacques said with a sad smile. "Another time."

When their food was ready, Jacques handed Scarlett her sack.

"Maybe I'll see you around the beach?"

"We come d-down about every d-day," Scarlett said. "Um, are you on Faceb-book?"

"Yeah, I am." Jacques said. "Just do a search for Jacques O'Larrity. I'm the only one on there."

Scarlett smiled. "I'll s-send you a friend request."

"That'd be cool," Jacques said.

"C'mon, Scarlett. Let's go," Kaitlynn called from the driver's seat of the pink Jeep.

Scarlett rolled her eyes, but shuffled over to the Jeep and climbed carefully into the passenger seat. She smiled at Jacques, and gave him a cute little wave before her sister spun gravel and pulled out onto Ocean Street.

Jacques led Ginger to a table near the back of the screened-in dining room so they could see the beach. They had to share a picnic table with a twenty-something couple. Jacques thought they might have been the couple who stopped at The Bean earlier, but he wasn't sure.

"Y'all mind if we sit down?" Jacques asked the young man.

The guy shrugged and said, "No problem. Help yourself."

The girl with him smiled and gestured to the empty seats.

Since it seemed like they really didn't mind, Jacques pointed to the seat that would give Ginger the best view of the ocean. He sat across from her.

Ginger took a bite of her burger. Juice dribbled down her chin. She grabbed a napkin from the stainless steel dispenser on the table to stop the juices from dripping onto her shirt.

Jacques laughed.

"I should have warned you. Iggie's burgers can be messy."

"So I noticed," Ginger said. "They're good though."

She took another bite, leaning carefully over the wrapper when she did so.

Lifting his cup, and shaking it a bit to test the thickness of his milkshake, Jacques took a tentative sip.

Ginger thought he looked a bit like a wine taster.

"How is it?"

Jacques wrinkled his nose. "Okay, I guess. Tastes like you'd expect a vanilla shake from a milkshake machine to taste."

He put his cup down and picked up an onion ring.

"You've got to try one of those onion rings." He pointed at the paper boat of onion rings Ginger pulled from her bag. "They're the best."

Ginger picked up an onion ring, gave it a good look, and then took a bite.

"Mmmm, it is good. I like how thin it is. Makes it really crispy."

Their conversation lagged as they enjoyed the food. When she'd eaten her last onion ring, Ginger shoved the grease stained paper boat back into the bag, and crumpled the bag into a small ball.

"So Jacques, I think you kind of liked Scarlett, didn't you?"

Her question caught Jacques just as he was sucking the last bit of milkshake up his straw. He coughed, shook his head, and tried to nonchalantly finish his shake.

Ginger cocked her head to one side, her eyes focused on him, her lip curled into an impish grin.

Jacques slowly lowered his cup to the table, pulled a napkin from the dispenser, and made a great show of carefully wiping his mouth. Ginger was not dissuaded. Her gaze never wavered. Jacques balled the napkin up and stuffed it into his bag.

"I don't know if I like her. I barely know her. We just met."

"Uh huh," Ginger said, shaking her head and giving Jacques a rueful grin. "You took one look into her eyes and forgot I was even here with you."

"What? No. I didn't forget you."

Ginger chuckled at Jacques's discomfort. Then she turned serious

"What do you think happened to her? How'd she get those scars? And what about her nose? It looked like it had been smashed flat and someone squeezed it back into shape."

Jacques wondered that himself. Scarlett was a pretty girl, even with the scars and all.

"We'll probably never know. I doubt I'll ever see her again."

Why that thought caused an empty feeling in his heart, Jacques couldn't say. He was confused about the feelings that meeting Scarlett invoked in him. He just met Ginger and really wanted her to like him, as maybe more than just a friend, but Ginger was right. When he'd met Scarlett, thoughts of Ginger disappeared from his mind altogether.

Sitting across from her at the table, Jacques realized Ginger had been right when she told Scarlett they were just good friends. While they might become close friends, his feelings for Ginger weren't anything like what he'd felt when he looked into Scarlett's eyes. Part of him regretted that. After all, Ginger was a good looking girl, but part of him acknowledged that the chemistry just wasn't there.

"What are you thinking about, JQ?" Ginger asked, seeing the far-away look in Jacques's eyes.

Jacques had no idea how to explain the thoughts running through his head to Ginger. Instead he said, "I'm thinking we should probably head back. Your dad's probably starting to wonder if you've forgotten about him. And I don't want to be late for Cienna's welcome back to the beach party."

Ginger had started to stand up, but stopped halfway out of her chair.

"What party? Who's Cienna?"

"Cienna is Mr. And Mrs. Philbert's granddaughter. She's coming out to stay with them a couple of weeks. She's been coming every summer since I can remember."

Seeing the confused frown on Ginger's face Jacques said, "The Philberts own The News Stand, the book store across the street from The Pari-Bean. Haven't you met them?"

Ginger put her hand over her mouth to stifle a laugh. "The Pari-Bean? Is that what you call the coffee shop?"

Jacques's face blanched in panic. "Oh, God. Please don't let my mother hear you call it that. She has a fit if she hears me say it."

Ginger shook her head, and lost her battle not to laugh.

"Okay… I promise… Marie won't hear it from me."

They walked to the bike rack, which was now full of bright green and orange bikes that hadn't there when Jacques and Ginger arrived at Iggie's. Ginger noticed a group of younger teens, wearing matching blue T-shirts, waiting in line to order food."

"Looks like some kind of youth group," she said, pointing out the kids to Jacques. "They must have cleaned Tony out of bikes."

Jacques counted how many Buzby Beach Bikes were in the rack besides Ginger's. "I only count seven. BB Bikes has a dozen or so cruisers. I wouldn't worry about it."

"Besides," Jacques said raising his brow suggestively, "I don't think Tony minds you riding one."

He expected Ginger to scoff at the idea. Instead, she turned a light shade of pink, and turned her head aside. Her reaction told Jacques he'd struck a chord. *Fair's fair after she picked on me about Scarlett.*

The ride back to The Bean wasn't as competitive as the ride to Iggie's had been. Where they could, they rode side by side.

"So, tell me more about this Cienna," Ginger said as they pedaled slowly up Eighth Street, past Dylan's Dive Shop and The Beach Emporium. "Do you and her have a a summer love thing going on?"

Jacques snorted. "It was nothing like that. We hung out together. She came into the shop every morning about ten for a frappacino, and hung out until I got off at noon. Then we biked to Iggie's for lunch, and hung out at the beach or something."

They stopped at the blinking red light where Eighth Street crossed Center Street. Ginger turned to Jacques and crossed her hands over her heart.

"You mean I'm not the first girl you've taken to Iggie's? JQ, I'm crushed." She tried to keep a sad face, but it was no use. She burst out laughing.

Jacques liked her using his nickname. It made him feel like they were really getting to be friends. He even liked how she was picking on him about Cienna.

Mr. Bishop was back when they returned the bright orange bike Ginger'd been riding.

"Tony's going to be sad he wasn't here. He told me all about you, young lady," Mr. Bishop said while he wheeled the bike into the back to be cleaned up before the next customer rode it.

Ginger smiled shyly. "He did? What did he say?"

"He told me the prettiest girl he'd ever seen on the island came by and borrowed a bike." Mr. Bishop narrowed his gaze. "Which he let her have on the house. I'll have to take it out of his pay."

"Oh don't do that, Mr. Bishop," Ginger said. "I'll pay for it. How much was it?"

Mr. Bishop chuckled and patted Ginger on the arm. "You'll do no such thing. You're no tourist, young lady. You're a neighbor, and a friend of JQ here. Consider it a favor to my landlord. I'll let Tony keep his hard earned money."

"Well, if you're sure?" Ginger said. She looked back and forth between Jacques and Mr. Bishop. "Tell Tony I'll see him later. He owes me a tour of the island."

Mr. Bishop laughed. "I'll be sure to tell him. That's one promise I'm sure my son will keep."

As they walked to The Beach Cone with Mr. Mumples now cold cheeseburger and onion rings,

Jacques said, "You know Tony's like nineteen, right? He just finished his first year of college."

Ginger turned to him and shrugged.

"So. It's not like I'm gonna go out with him. We're just gonna ride bikes around the island. If I'm gonna live here, I should know my way around."

Jacques said, "I could show you around the island. I've lived here all my life. Mr. Bishop just bought the bike shop four years ago. They're from New Jersey."

Ginger stopped and glared at Jacques. "What's wrong with people from New Jersey?"

Jacques took a step away from her glare. "Nothing. I like the Bishop's, a lot. Really. I just meant that I know the island better than Tony. That's all."

Ginger pursed her lips and tilted her head. "You're not jealous are you?" she asked, arching her brow repeatedly.

Jacques laughed. "Deathly so," he said, grabbing his chest. "I could just die."

Ginger punched him on the arm. "You're crazy. The only reason you want to show me around the island is so you can find Scarlett."

"Maybe," Jacques said.

"I knew you liked her," Ginger said.

She stuck her tongue out at Jacques and darted through the door to The Beach Cone.

While Mr. Mumples ate his lunch - reheated in the ice cream shop's new microwave - Ginger gave Jacques a tour of the place. The tour concluded in the storage room Ginger had been working in when Jacques arrived to take her to lunch.

"My dad's got me organizing all the supplies back here. He gave me a list of how he thinks things should be set up, but I'm not sure about some of his ideas."

Jacques studied the list and the layout of the storage room. "I've helped my mom and Kelly organize inventory next door. Maybe I could help you."

CHAPTER FIVE

Before Ginger could reply, Marie's ring tone began playing on Jacques's phone. He pulled the phone from his back pocket and slid his fingertip across the screen to unlock it before putting it to his ear.

"Hi, Mom." Jacques listened for a moment and then said, "Okay. I'll head right over. Thanks. Love you."

He touched the screen to end the call, pushed the sleep button on top of the phone, and slid it back into his pocket.

"That was my mom."

"Cool ring tone.' Was that Brooks and Dunn?"

"Yeah," Jacques said, impressed she'd know that.

"I gotta go. Mrs. Philbert called the coffee shop to let me know that Cienna's parents were almost to the drawbridge."

When he saw the disappointed look on Ginger's face, he said, "Hey, why don't you come, too? I know they won't mind, and you'd like Cienna. She's pretty cool."

Ginger ached to go, but she couldn't.

"My dad really needs me to finish this up. He says we're opening tomorrow at noon, no matter what. I'd better stay."

Jacques looked around the storage room, taking in the amount of work still to be done. He felt pulled in two directions. Part of him couldn't wait to see Cienna again, but part of him wanted to stay and help Ginger.

Sensing his dilemma Ginger said, "You go and see your friend. I mean, it's been a year, right? Me and these boxes will still be here if you want to stop by later."

Jacques felt relieved, though a little guilt nagged at him for deserting Ginger.

"Okay, I'll stop by later. And I'll see if Cienna wants to come, too. If all of us pitch in, it'll get done in no time."

Ginger doubted Cienna would be interested in helping out, but she smiled at Jacques.

"That would be great."

Cienna's folks pulled up outside The News Stand in their rented SUV just minutes after Jacques walked in the door.

Jacques turned toward the door when the bell jangled. Reginald Philbert, Cienna's father, stood in the doorway holding the door open for his wife, Soon Lee, Cienna, and Cienna's little brother, Brandon. Brandon was ten years younger than Cienna. Reginald met and married Soon Lee during his first tour in Korea in the early 1990's.

Reginald's six-foot four-inch frame towered over Soon Lee's petite five-foot-two. Fortunately for Cienna, she'd inherited some of her father's height and, Jacques noted, had obviously had a growth spurt since the summer before. She now stood a good five inches taller than her mother.

Jacques stood open mouthed, looking at Cienna as she came through the door. Though she looked familiar, the girl he'd hung out with over summers past had been replaced by a beautiful young lady. Her straight black hair, which once reached past her shoulders, was cut into a fashionable pageboy style, accenting a face that had lost much of its childish roundness.

Cienna spotted Jacques and smiled, revealing teeth constrained by braces complete with blue and green bands. Seeing hers, Jacques's tongue ran over the bands and wires that adorned his own teeth. He smiled back at her. Cienna hadn't worn braces last year.

Jacques was about to say "Hi" when Mrs. Philbert burst out with, "There you are," and came at as near a run as she ever got to greet her son and his family. Mr. Philbert wasn't far behind. Jacques was forgotten for the moment as the family exchanged hugs and kisses.

The cake Marie decorated for Cienna's return was served in the reading room since it had a big oak conference table with eight captain's chairs on wheels around it. The Buzby Beach Book Club met there every Thursday at noon to share lunch and talk about the newest book they were reading. Jacques sniffed; certain he could still smell the ladies' perfume.

Brandon polished off his first piece of cake. "Grandma, can I have another?"

Soon Lee clucked disapprovingly. "I think one is enough, Brandon."

Brandon looked his dad, hoping to win on appeal.

Reginald's eyes narrowed. "Your mother said one is enough, son."

Mrs. Philbert looked like she was about to argue, but an unspoken warning in the way Mr. Philbert raised his brow when he caught her eye stopped her.

Cienna put her mouth close to Jacques's ear, and said, "My mom's always worried about Brandon eating too much. It's not like he's fat."

Jacques barely heard the words. His skin warmed and his heart raced at the proximity of her lips to his face.

"Uh huh, he's not like fat," Jacques stammered.

Cienna gave Jacques a funny look.

"Okay. Anyway. How are things at the coffee shop? Your mom staying busy? I can't wait to see Marie again."

"Things are going well at The Bean. Did you know The Sand Bar closed?"

Cienna swallowed her last bite of cake before answering. "I think you posted something about that on Facebook a while back. Is it opening back up for the summer?"

Jacques downed the last of his fruit punch.

"Not as a bar. Mr. Mumples is opening up an ice cream shop in there. He's supposed to open tomorrow."

"An ice cream place," Cienna said. "That's cool." She snorted and rolled her eyes. "Ice cream's cool. Can't believe I said that."

"Mr. Mumples is a nice guy. And Ginger, that's his daughter, she's pretty cool."

Cienna sat back in her chair, eyes wide. "Ginger, huh? Did my JQ find a girlfriend while I was away?"

A hint of something that might have been worry, or jealousy, crept into Cienna's voice, but Jacques missed it. He just shook his head.

"It's not like that. We just met this morning when she came in to get a latte. I took her to Iggie's for lunch and we rode bikes. No big deal."

Cienna lowered her chin and looked at Jacques through long, delicate lashes. "You just met her and you already had a lunch date. Sounds like a big deal to me."

Jacques, finally clueing to the idea Cienna might be jealous, sought to reassure her that he and Ginger weren't a couple.

"No, not really. We're just friends. Like I said, she just arrived on the island and I was showing her around."

Cienna's eyes narrowed and her lips turned down in a pouty frown.

"Okay. Whatever you say. So when do I get to meet your friend Ginger?"

Jacques pushed his glasses up his nose, rubbed his chin, and finally folded his hands on the table.

"She's probably still at The Beach Cone helping her dad get ready for tomorrow. We could go over there now, if it's okay with your parents."

Jacques was not expecting the reaction he got from Ginger when he walked into The Beach Cone with Cienna. The smile that started forming on Ginger's lips when Jacques knocked on the door frame disappeared when she saw Cienna standing behind him. Ginger stood up and brushed her hands on the front of her shorts.

"Hi, JQ. I guess this is Cienna."

Ginger's tone was somewhat shy of friendly.

Jacques looked from Ginger to Cienna, and back to Ginger. It looked to him like the two girls were sizing each other up. He felt a light sheen of sweat break out on his forehead. "Um, yeah, Ginger, this is Cienna. I told you about her coming to stay with the Philberts."

He turned to Cienna. "Cienna, this is Ginger. You met her dad out front. Ginger just moved here."

Cienna's nearly black eyes scanned Ginger from her disheveled reddish-brown hair down to her dirty white canvas sneakers. Ginger's forest green eyes did the same to Cienna, from her night black hair to her sling-back sandals. Examination complete, both girls raised their heads until their eyes met.

For one long second, they looked at each other. Standing uncomfortably between them, Jacques felt a cold bead of sweat roll between his shoulder blades and continue down to the waistband of his cargo shorts. He wanted to say something, anything, to break the tension, but his mouth was dry and his mind was blank.

Suddenly, as if in response to some secret signal, both girls smiled. "Nice to meet ya," Ginger said. "How long you gonna be around?"

Cienna pushed past Jacques before answering. "A couple of weeks, maybe longer. Not sure yet."

Cienna looked around the storage room Ginger was organizing.

"Looks like you've been hard at it."

Ginger shook her head, and said, "Girl, you're not kidding. But we're just about ready. Looks like we'll be open tomorrow right on time. Well, actually a week late. Let me show you around."

Ginger took Cienna by the hand and led her to the front of the store. Jacques stood there wondering if they'd forgotten he was there until Ginger turned and looked over Cienna's shoulder.

"You coming, JQ?"

"Sure," Jacques said, with a crooked frown. "What else have I got to do?"

Ginger gave Cienna a quick tour of the ice cream shop, and then they disappeared into the storage room. A short time later they headed right past Mr. Mumples and out the door.

Jacques stopped to help Mr. Mumples pick up the last of the painting supplies and equipment and wound up staying to help clean up. They scrubbed down the service counter and then, while Mr. Mumples filled the cup dispensers behind the counter, Jacques swept the customer seating area.

"I guess you're all set for tomorrow," Jacques said after emptying the dust pan into the trash can.

"As ready as we can be," Mr. Mumples replied. "I'm glad Ella Rue has tomorrow off so she can help out. If we're lucky, we'll be so busy tomorrow it'll take all three of us to keep up."

"If you want, I can come over and help when I get done at The Bean," Jacques said.

"I appreciate it, Jacques," Mr. Mumples said. He'd not taken to calling Jacques JQ. "But I think between the three of us, we'll be okay."

"Then I'll definitely come over and have some ice cream," Jacques said. "Having you guys next door will sure be more fun than that old bar."

The sharp electronic "bing-bing" of the door buzzer announced that Ginger and Cienna were back.

"Where did you two get off to?" Mr. Mumples asked.

Ginger, not the least intimidated by her father's stern expression said, "Cienna took me over to The News Stand to meet her parents and grandparents."

"Mm, hmm," Mr. Mumples said, scratching his chin. "Before you left, did you happen to finish arranging the storage room like I asked?"

Ginger rose on her toes and kissed her dad's cheek. His five o'clock shadow was rough on her lips.

"Yes, Daddy. It's all in order and everything is put away. Cienna helped me finish up." She turned an accusing eye on Jacques.

"Someone else was supposed to help me, but he kind of disappeared."

"Jacques was out here helping me finish getting the front ready," Mr. Mumples said. "Thanks to him all we need to do now is show up tomorrow and get everything ready for customers to come in and start eating ice cream."

The door "bing-binged" again and Mrs. Mumples walked in. Jacques thought Ginger's mom looked like an older version of his new friend.

"Then," Mrs. Mumples said, "I think we need to celebrate with dinner on the town. What do you say?"

"I say let's do it," Mr. Mumples said, taking his wife in his arms for a hug.

"Sounds like a plan," Ginger said, joining in the hug.

Jacques concentrated intently on the mirror behind the counter. Cienna developed a sudden interest in the neon ice cream cone in the window.

Ginger nudged her head against her dad's shoulder, and then nodded toward her two friends.

Mr. Mumples scratched his head and nodded. "Of course our two biggest helpers are invited, right dear?"

Mrs. Mumples brow furrowed, and her frown plainly showed her plan was for a family dinner, but she said, "Of course, dear. I'm sure they've worked hard enough to have earned dinner."

Neither Jacques nor Cienna were fooled by her words. Mrs. Mumples' tone made it clear that she doubted they'd worked hard enough to warrant being taken to dinner.

Jacques cleared his throat. "Thanks just the same, but my mom and I always go to Mama Leone's for pizza on Friday night. It's kind of a tradition."

Cienna begged off, too. "My grandparents are taking us all out to The Trident. It's my dad's favorite restaurant on the island."

Ginger's face crumpled in disappointment.

Mrs. Mumples expression brightened with relief.

Mr. Mumples said, "Well, some other time, then."

After one last check around the shop, Mr. Mumples locked up and the family headed home, which was only half-a-mile away. They left in two vehicles, Ginger and Mrs. Mumples in her Lexus, Mr. Mumples in his F-150 4x4.

"I'd like a truck like that," Jacques said. "Four wheel drive and all."

"I'd rather have a Jeep," Cienna said. "A Wrangler, with big tires for riding on the beach."

Her mention of a Jeep made Jacques think of Kaitlynn's Jeep and he wondered if Scarlett was still at the beach. As if his thinking about them caused them to appear, a horn sounded and he heard someone call his name.

"Hey Jack," Kaitlynn shouted from across the road. "Coffee any good at that Bean place?"

Jacques, ignoring her mispronunciation of his name, hollered back, "Best coffee on the island."

"Humph," Kaitlynn said, putting the Jeep back in gear. "We'll see in the morning."

She drove off toward the drawbridge. Jacques caught a glimpse of Scarlett waving to him from the passenger seat. His heart rate sped up just a touch at the sight. *I hope she really comes tomorrow.*

Cienna was giving him a puzzled look.

"Who was that? Friends of yours?"

She didn't sound like she thought they were friends.

"Just some girls Ginger and I met at Iggie's at lunch. Kaitlynn, the girl driving, almost ran me over in front of the bike shop."

Cienna snorted a sharp laugh. "Maybe you should put salt in her coffee, if she shows up tomorrow."

Jacques raised his eyebrow and thought about it for a moment. Then he shook his head, and said, "Kelly actually found a new espresso recipe where you sprinkle sea salt on top of the whipped cream before you drizzle on the syrup."

Cienna wrinkled her nose. "That doesn't sound like it would be very good."

"I didn't think so either," Jacques said. "But it's not bad. Kind of salty-sweet, like a chocolate covered pretzel. Lots of people have tried it and liked it."

"Maybe I'll give it a try some time," Cienna said before pulling her cell phone out of her pocket and checking the time. "Oops, I'd better go."

Even as the words left her mouth, her father appeared at the door of The News Stand. Seeing Cienna standing there with Jacques, he waved and signaled that she should come on.

Cienna waved back, and nodded .

Turning to Jacques, she said, "It's great to see you again, JQ. I missed you." She surprised him with a quick hug before darting across the road.

Standing alone on the sidewalk, Jacques took a deep breath and let it out slowly. It had been a long, and very interesting, first day of summer break. And there was still pizza to come.

CHAPTER SIX

Jacques' eyes were jarred open by Trace Adkins, "Brown Chicken Brown Cow" dark and early the next morning. His arm snaked across his bed, stalking the snooze button, but before he could hit it, his mother knocked on his door.

"I'm already up, honey. Take your time. I'll meet you down stairs."

Jacques blinked his eyes, and stared at his clock/radio. 4:01 stared back at him.

"Stupid alarm clock."

An hour later - showered, dressed, and slightly more awake - Jacques stood at the front door of The Parisian Bean, wondering why the lights were already on in the back. He squeezed his eyes shut, counted to five in his head, and opened them again. *The lights are on because*

Mom's got that big cupcake order for that thing down at The Coastal Tower.

Jacques turned the knob and started to push the door open when footsteps on the sidewalk caused him to stop and look toward The Beach Cone. It wasn't, as he'd hoped it would be, Ginger. Ginger was, at that moment, lacing on her running shoes prior to heading out to put in some miles on the beach.

Most people would have felt a moments panic seeing the figure that came into sight under the dim street light. The shaggy brown hair, the unkempt beard, the threadbare-sleeveless denim shirt, the ragged cut-off jean shorts, and the worn flip-flops, did not mark Scout as one of Buzby Beach's upper crust.

No one was quite sure where Scout came from. His accent was hard to pin down. He once told Jacques, on one of those rare occasions when Scout was feeling talkative, that his accent was the Yankee-Rebel-Midwestern-Pacific Coast-Brooklyn sound that guys get after being in the Army long enough. Usually, all Jacques heard from Scout was his coffee order.

"Morning, Scout. I'm afraid you're too early for coffee. We're not open yet."

"Not a problem," Scout said so softly Jacques could barely hear him. "I'll wait."

Scout was an enigma to the people on the island. He'd shown up half-a-dozen years earlier, taken a room at Come-N-Stay Rooms and Apartments, and he'd been there ever since. While he took odd jobs around the island once in a while, he spent most of his days at the north end of the island surfing or surf fishing.

Jacques stopped partway through the door.

"Hey Scout, you want to wait inside?"

Scout straightened up from the light pole he'd been leaning on."Sure."

He followed Jacques into The Bean and took a seat near the window.

The aroma of coffee brewing filled the café. Jacques could hear the mixer at work in the kitchen. He glanced at Scout sitting there by the window, staring intently out into the dimly lit street, and decided he should let his mom know he'd let the guy in to wait.

Jacques didn't think Marie would mind. Scout was a regular customer. While not a native to the island, he was a year-round resident, and as such, a de facto member of the unofficial club.

Marie looked up when Jacques knocked on the door frame.

"Good morning, JQ. Ready for a busy day?"

"Yes, ma'am," Jacques said. He glanced over his shoulder toward the front of the cafe. "Uh, I let Scout in to wait. Didn't seem right to let him stand out on the walk until six."

"That's okay. Scout's okay. Did you get him a cup of coffee? I started some regular brewing. It should be ready by now."

"No, I didn't," Jacques said, "but I will. I just wanted to let you know he was here."

"It's good you did. Now, shoo. I've got to get these cupcakes done." Marie blew him a kiss as he backed out the door.

Scout was still sitting looking out the window. The sky was starting to lighten. Jacques wondered what Scout thought about as he looked out the window.

"Hey, Scout. We've got coffee ready if you'd like some. House blend, black, right?"

Scout nodded his head, without ever shifting his gaze. "Thanks."

Mr. Philbert once told Jacques that Scout was an Afghanistan vet.

"I think he was a Ranger or something like that," Mr. Philbert had said. "Those guys saw some things you couldn't imagine, Jacques."

Jacques knew Mr. Philbert spent time in Vietnam. He had a slight limp for a souvenir of the eleven months he'd spent in country, but Jacques learned that from Mrs. Philbert. Mr. Philbert never talked about it, at least not with Jacques.

Joe showed up with the bakery delivery about the time Jacques handed Scout his coffee.

"Good morning, Mr. Bagley," Jacques said as he opened the door for Joe. "Bet it's a big order this morning."

Joe laughed and patted Jacques shoulder."You got that right."

His expression became puzzled when he saw someone sitting by the window. "Morning, Scout. How're you this morning?"

Scout set his cup down carefully and stood. "Good morning, Joe. Need a hand?"

Joe smiled. "Could always use a hand. Thanks."

It didn't take Joe and Scout long to bring in the order. While they did, Jacques got Joe's coffee ready. Marie, hearing the commotion, came out of the kitchen to say hello.

"Good morning, Joe. See you got yourself some help this morning," Marie said, before turning to Scout. "Good morning, Scout. You're out early." Scout's nod was nearly a bow.

"Ma'am."

"I see you're up early, Marie," Joe said. "I thought you turned over the early work to Jacques."

"Big order for that conference down at the Tower. Speaking of which, I'd better get back to it. Y'all have a good one."

She rubbed Jacques' head on her way back to the kitchen.

Jacques noticed Scout's eyes following Marie until she disappeared through the hall door. Scout sighed and returned to his table. Joe went over and spoke to him quietly. Jacques thought he saw Joe put a couple of bills in Scout's hand, but he couldn't be sure.

Six o'clock arrived and with it, Mrs. Philbert and Cienna's mom, Soon Lee.

Jacques looked out the door to see if Cienna might be following them.

Mrs. Philbert noticed, and chuckled.

"Sorry to disappoint you, Jacques, but Cienna's sleeping in this morning. Herbert's going to mind the store while Soon Lee and I go for a walk on the beach."

From then, the morning proceeded much like every other summer morning, perhaps busier than some due to it being Saturday. Jacques kept hoping to see Ginger come in, but she must have been too busy helping her mom and dad get things ready for the grand opening of The Beach Cone next door.

Kelly showed up at her usual time, just as the Nine O'Clock Club showed up. The ladies in the Nine O'Clock Club showed up seven days a week. They might not all make it every time, but those that could, did.

On the heels of the Nine O'Clock Club came the four girls from the pink Jeep incident, Scarlett, Kaitlynn, Trish, and Marissa. Kaitlynn stopped just inside the door, took a look around the café, and nodded approvingly. Scarlett watched her sister's appraisal, and then looked at Jacques behind the counter, smiled, and rolled her eyes.

While Kelly waited on the Nine O'Clock Club, Jacques helped the couple of customers in line ahead of Scarlett and her posse. Each time he returned to the counter, his eyes were drawn to Scarlett's. She seemed to be watching his every move with great interest. Jacques was flattered, but the scrutiny also made him a little nervous.

Finally, it was the girls' turn.

Kaitlynn studied the menu, her lips twisting into a frown. "I'm not sure what to try."

She put her hands on her hips, thrust her shoulders forward, and looked at Jacques."What do you recommend, Daredevil?"

Jacques tried very hard to ignore how her black bikini top was clearly visible through her tight, white t-shirt, and recommended his favorite espresso drink.

"My favorite is a caramel macchiato. If you like white chocolate, I make a delicious white chocolate mocha."

"I absolutely love white chocolate," Kaitlynn said. "I'll have one of those."

"How big would you like it?" Jacques asked.

"What's your biggest size?" Kaitlynn asked.

When Jacques showed her a Buzby Bucket she said, "Oh God, no. That's too much. If that's a large, I'll take a medium."

Jacque prepared her a twenty ounce white chocolate mocha. Trish was next.

"I'd like a decaf, low-fat, sugar free, caramel latte," Trish said. "The same size as Kaitlynn's."

"Coming right up," Jacques said, turning to prepare Trish's order.

When he handed it to her, she took a sip and asked, "This is decaf?"

"It sure is," Jacques said. "Our beans are roasted fresh over in Wilmington each week. Our decaf is better than most places regular coffee."

Trish took another sip. "It is very good."

Marissa stepped up to the counter. Jacques glanced over her shoulder at Scarlett and was rewarded with a smile.

Marissa said, "My order is easy. I'll take one of those Bucket's full of regular coffee, two shots of cream, and two shots of peppermint."

Jacques' brows went up. "You sure you want a Bucket."

Marissa nodded. "Oh, yeah. I'm a caffeine fiend."

She laughed softly at her own play on words.

"Coming right up," Jacques said.

He filled the Bucket up half-way, added the cream and peppermint syrup, and then topped it off.

He handed it to Marissa saying, "One Buzby Bucket, two creams, and two peppermints. Enjoy."

Marissa sniffed the steam rising from the opening in the lid before taking a sip."Oh, I will. Thanks."

At last it was Scarlett's turn. Her t-shirt didn't fit as tightly as her sister's, but Jacques could see she was wearing a shimmering blue, one-piece bathing suit under it. He brought his gaze up to meet her eyes, her beautiful gray-green eyes, and swallowed hard.

Scarlett's expression told Jacques she'd noticed him checking her out, but she didn't look angry. Amused would be more like it. Perhaps even pleased.

"I'm not a b-big c-coffee drinker," Scarlett said softly. "But I think I'll t-try one of those c-caramel things you t-told K-kaitlynn about."

"A caramel macchiato?" Jacques asked.

"Yeah," Scarlett said. "Let me t-try one of those."

"I'll make you a small one, on me, so you can see if you like it," Jacques said.

"Oh, okay. Th-thanks," Scarlett said, giving him another smile.

Jacques noticed again that Scarlett only seemed to be able to smile with half her mouth. *I wonder how she got those scars?*

He took great care in preparing Scarlett's small espresso. It was important to him that she like it. When it was ready, he presented it to her with a slight bow.

"Your caramel macchiato, my lady."

Scarlett laughed lightly at his formal presentation. Her laughter tickled the inside of his ears, drew his lips into a smile, and warmed a place in his heart, all at once. She picked up the cup and sniffed the steam coming out the opening in the lid.

"It's very hot," she said.

Jacques' hands were shaking. The last thing he wanted was for her to burn her lips or tongue.

"Yes. The whipped cream helps cool it off, but it's still pretty hot. Sip it carefully."

Scarlett tilted the cup ever so slowly, allowing just a drop to escape onto her tongue. Satisfied that she hadn't scalded herself, she took a bigger sip.

"This is very good. It tastes kind of like a Milky Way bar. Now I wish I'd gotten a larger one."

"If you finish that one and still want more, I'll make you another one," Jacques said.

"Okay," Scarlett said. "By the way, did you get my friend request on Facebook?"

Jacques bit his lip. "I'm sorry. I haven't even checked my Facebook since yesterday. My mom and I went out for dinner, and then caught a movie, and by the time I got home it was late and I had to be up early and -"

"It's okay," Scarlett said.

She handed him a piece of paper. "Here's my cell number. Text me, okay?"

Jacques felt lightheaded, and he almost dropped the slip of paper with her number on it. "Okay."

The door bells rang as another customer entered the store. "I'd better go sit down. You've got customers waiting."

"Okay."

He waited on several more customers, and had just taken an order for a double chocolate mocha, when he noticed Scarlett and the other girls getting up to leave.

"Excuse me just a moment," Jacques said to the double chocolate mocha customer. "I'll be right back."

Trish and Marissa were already out the door. Kaitlynn held the door open, waiting for Scarlett to make her way slowly there. Jacques eyed the situation, and headed for the door.

"I've got it," he said to Kaitlynn.

Kaitlynn tilted her head and gave him a puzzled grin, but moved away so he could hold the door open for Scarlett.

"So, uhm, you guys are gonna be on the beach?" Jacques asked.

Scarlett squinted one eye and focused on him with the other. "Hence the b-bathing suits."

Jacques couldn't help but smile. "Did you really just say 'hence'?"

"I g-guess I d-did," Scarlett said. "Where d-did you think we were g-gonna g-go?"

"Uhm, I mean, I knew you were going to the beach. I meant, where at the beach are you going?"

Jacques grimaced and shook his head. "Uh, never mind."

Scarlett felt her heart flutter. "We'll b-be near the p-pier, across from Shirley's."

"I know where that is," Jacques said. "Maybe I'll see you down there."

"That'd b-be c-cool," Scarlett said.

Out of the corner of his eye, Jacques caught sight of the double chocolate mocha customer watching him.

"I'd better get back to work. See you later?"

"I hope so," Scarlett said, dropping her gaze shyly, but then raising her eyes to meet Jacques'.

Once in the Jeep, Kaitlynn asked, "What was that all about?"

"Jacques wanted t-to know if he c-could meet me on the b-beach later," Scarlett said, a light blush coloring her cheeks. But she couldn't stop grinning.

Kaitlynn looked in the through the café window at Jacques handing the customer his double chocolate mocha.

"Cool. Daredevil seems like a nice kid. He definitely likes you, Scar."

Jacques watched the pink Jeep pull away and then checked the clock on the wall below the menu board behind the counter. There was still another two hours before Cameron's shift started and he could leave. Jacques figured he'd grab a burger at Iggie's, or maybe find Scarlett first and see if she wanted to have lunch with him.

Even as he was picturing himself sitting in Iggie's screened-in dining room with Scarlett, Ginger and

Cienna walked in the door together. Ginger had a handful of papers.

"Hi JQ," Ginger said, holding out one of the papers to Jacques. "My dad told me to ask your mom if we could hand out these fliers to your customers."

Kelly stepped up to the counter, and said, "Let me see those."

Ginger handed Kelly the fliers. "They're to announce our grand opening at noon today. The Beach Cone's finally opening for business."

Kelly gave Ginger the fliers back. "I don't think Marie will mind. She's down at the Tower delivering cupcakes."

Jacques took one of the fliers and read it with a sinking feeling in the pit of his stomach. He'd forgotten all about The Beach Cone's grand opening. Of course he had to be there for it. Not just because he and Ginger were becoming friends, but they were right next door and it would be the neighborly thing to do. Jacques knew what his mom would say.

Ginger tugged at the flier in Jacques' hand. "You know all about it. I already know you're coming."

Jacques relinquished the flier. "I'll be there all right. Wouldn't miss it."

Though he tried to sound enthused about the idea, the way Cienna narrowed her eyes at him told Jacques he might not have pulled it off. Ginger didn't seem to notice as she circulated among the customers seated around the cafe, handing out fliers.

When Cameron came in at noon, Jacques went up to the apartment to clean up before heading next door the The Beach Cone. He quickly checked his Facebook account and responded to Scarlett's friend request, feeling just a twinge of guilt that he hadn't checked it the night before.

Wearing a clean Parisian Bean golf shirt, Carolina Blue - though he was a State fan - and a fresh pair of cargo shorts, he headed down to The Beach Cone.

"Everyone calls the coffee shop The Bean," he said to himself as he rushed down the stairs two-at-a-time. "Won't be long before they start calling The Beach Cone, The Cone." He rounded the corner of the building by Buzby Beach Bikes and nearly ran into Tony.

"Whoa, Jacques. What's the hurry?" Tony asked.

"No hurry. Just heading over to The Cone for the big grand opening," Jacques said.

He figured he might as well be the first to start calling it The Cone.

"I was headed that way too," Tony said. "My dad's letting me take a long lunch break so I can hang out over there a while. I didn't think he was gonna, but Ginger talked him into it."

Jacques felt a twinge of jealousy, but quickly suppressed it. After all, it wasn't like he liked Ginger that way.

"Then we'd better get going," Jacques said. "They've probably already opened the doors."

CHAPTER SEVEN

Jacques and Tony hadn't missed it. Jasper Krispich, Mayor of the Town of Buzby Beach, was wrapping up his speech as they walked up. Jacques saw Nancy Bitterman, the President of the Buzby Beach Chamber of Commerce, standing beside the mayor. He hadn't realized the opening of an ice cream parlor was such a big deal.

The Mumples were standing on the other side of the mayor and there was a big rainbow colored ribbon strung across the entrance to The Beach Cone. Jacques figured there must be twenty or thirty people standing around waiting for the ribbon cutting. Tony nudged him and pointed to a van parked nearby with WECT-TV6 painted on the side.

Ginger spotted Tony standing near the back of the crowd. At just over six feet, Tony was hard to miss. She stood on tip-toe and whispered something in Mr. Mumples' ear. AW, as Mr. Mumples was called - it stood for Atwater Winthrop - caught Tony's eye, and with a nod of his head signaled that Tony should move up front and join them.

Tony grabbed Jacques' arm and said, "C'mon. They want us up there with them."

Jacques hesitated. "I don't know. He was just looking at you."

Tony tugged again. "C'mon. He meant us both."

Jacques gave in and pushed his way to the front with Tony. Ginger smiled at Tony when they moved around to stand next to her and her mom. She looked at Jacques and gave him a slight nod.

Jacques made a face and nodded back. He felt someone nudge him from behind. Turning he noticed Cienna.

Where did she come from? I didn't see her standing up here.

Cienna leaned her head close and whispered, "You be nice. She's nervous enough with the TV cameras and everything."

Jacques felt that warm tingling again, with Cienna's lips so close to his ear. He turned and gave her a shaky smile.

"I'll behave," he mouthed.

"You better," Cienna mouthed back.

The mayor finished his speech about how glad he was to welcome a new business to town. Polite applause acknowledged how glad everyone was that he'd stopped talking.

Nancy Bitterman handed the three-foot long pair of scissors kept on hand at the Chamber of Commerce office for just such occasions to Mr. Mumples. He in turn handed the oversized scissors to Ginger and Mrs. Mumples who, once the cameras were on them and the photographer from the Wilmington Star News was ready, used the scissors to cut the rainbow colored ribbon.

The ribbon came apart easily, thanks to some preparation beforehand. The successful cutting was greeted with a round of applause much more enthusiastic than that which greeted the end of the mayor's speech. A proudly beaming Mr. Mumples then opened the door and announced that The Beach Cone was in business.

Mr. Mumples stood aside and motioned Mayor Krispich and Ms. Bitterman inside. Mrs. Mumples and Ginger followed them. Ginger took her station behind the counter, putting on her white painter's hat, adorned with The Beach Cone logo across the front, and took the Mayor's and Ms. Bitterman's orders.

"Make mine a double scoop of mint chocolate chip in a waffle cone," the mayor said.

"Coming right up sir," Ginger replied with a smile. "And you, ma'am?"

"Hmm, I think I'll take a single scoop of butter pecan in a plain cone," Ms. Bitterman said. "Gotta watch my figure, don't you know."

Ms. Bitterman's buxom figure was probably being watched by several of the men in attendance. Twice divorced, Nancy never lacked for male attention.

Tony, Cienna, and Jacques filed into The Cone along with the television news crew, the photographer from the Star News, and about a dozen others. The seating area of The Cone could have held more, but not many more. While Ginger and her folks made cones, sundaes, and Gyrations - a blended concoction of soft-serve vanilla and your choice of candy or cookies - Tony, Cienna, and Jacques took a table by the front window far from the door.

The commotion in the store made conversation difficult. Instead of trying to talk over it, Jacques pulled out his cell phone and sent Scarlett a text.

What r u guys doing for lunch? Iggie's?

He didn't know whether or not Scarlett had her phone with her and turned on while she was on the beach. After a couple of minutes passed without a reply, he put the phone back in his pocket.

Cienna was eyeing him suspiciously. She asked loud enough to be heard over the noise, "Who were you texting?"

Jacques bit his lip, trying to decide what to tell Cienna about Scarlett when his phone beeped to indicate an incoming message.

We r still catchin rays. R u still working?

Jacques ignored Cienna's inquisitive look.

No. Am at Beach Cone 4 grand opening.

Oh. wheres that?

Cienna was leaning over his shoulder, trying to see who he was texting.

"It's just a friend of mine, okay," he said, turning away before typing,

Right next to Bean. Just opened today. Gingers dad owns it.

Your g/f dad?

Jacques felt heat rise in his cheeks. He didn't want Scarlett thinking Ginger was his girlfriend.

Ginger not my g/f. Just/f.

Just/f. lol. Good.

Jacques tilted his head and looked at the screen.

"Whoever it is thinks it's good that you and Ginger are just friends," Cienna said over his shoulder.

"Hey," Jacques said, "this is private."

He turned to glare at Cienna and noticed Tony was no longer at the table.

"He's at the counter getting an ice cream from your 'just friend,' Cienna said, her voice rife with sarcasm. "I think he wants to be more than just friends with her."

"That's cool," Jacques said. "Tony's a good guy. She could do worse."

Cienna gnawed at her lower lip and stared at Jacques through narrowed eyes. Jacques chewed his lip in imitation of her and stared back. It worked. Cienna started laughing.

"I like Ginger, Cienna, but I don't think there's romance in our future."

Cienna turned to see Ginger touch Tony lightly on the arm as she handed him his double scoop of cookies-and-cream in a chocolate lined waffle cone.

"Looks like you're right about that. I think bicycle boy has got all her attention." Jacques saw the way Ginger was looking at Tony and nodded.

"What about you and your boyfriend, Cienna? Your FB status never changed so I assume you and Josh are still together."

Cienna sat back, a sad look on her face. "At least for now."

"Why just for now?"

Cienna looked out the window at The News Stand across the street. Without turning around, she said, "My dad's got orders for Korea. He's leaving at the end of summer. We're not going with him this time. It's just for a year, and then he's gonna retire."

She said it so softly, if the commotion hadn't died down so much, Jacques wouldn't have heard her.

"If you're not going with him, and that's a bummer, I know, why do you have to break up with Josh?"

Cienna turned back toward him. "Because Brandon, me, and my mom are moving here when he leaves. We're gonna live here after he retires. That rental house my dad owns over on Fourth Street. That's where we're gonna live."

Jacques thought that was good news. "Hey, then we'll get to hang out together. And that's right around the corner from Ginger's house. You'll go to my school. You both will if Ginger decides to stay. And you'll get to see your grandparents all the time. It'll be great."

Cienna forced a smile. "Maybe you're right. I suppose it has its good points."

She pushed away from the table and stood. "Think I'll go get some ice cream. How 'bout you, JQ?"

"I'll be over there in a minute," Jacques said, picking his phone up from the table.

Cienna nodded and walked over to the counter, getting there just as Tony walked out.

Jacques looked at his screen. There was a new message from Scarlett.

We r gonna get lunch soon. U b able to meet @ Iggies?

A few minutes before, Jacques would have keyed back a yes without a thought, but now there was a thought; the thought of Cienna moving to the island to stay. Knowing she had a boyfriend back home had always kept her solidly in the "just friends camp." Now he had to wonder. He didn't want to keep Scarlett wondering, though. She was someone he definitely wanted to get to know better.

B there in 30 mins.

CHAPTER EIGHT

Not wanting to spoil his lunch, Jacques ordered a single scoop of vanilla in a plain cone.

"You're kidding me," Ginger said. "That's all you want?"

Jacques explained. "And I'll take it to go. I've got a lunch date."

Ginger smiled. Cienna's expression was neutral, hiding the irritation she felt. After what she'd just shared with him, Cienna couldn't believe Jacques was rushing off to be with some other girl.

Oblivious to Cienna's irritation, Jacques ate his cone as he walked down the block to Buzby Beach Bikes to pick up his beach cruiser. He made it to Iggie's twenty-eight minutes after his last text to Scarlett.

Scarlett was sitting alone at an outdoor table near the road, watching for him.

"Kaitlynn and the others already g-got their food. I waited for you."

"I'm glad you waited," Jacques replied as he plopped down on the seat next to her. "Is Kaitlynn going to give you a hard time about waiting around to ride back?" Scarlett shook her head.

"She d-didn't want t-to lose her p-parking space, so we walked."

As if she knew what Jacques was about to say next, Scarlett said, "They g-gave me a head start. I c-can walk, you know. I j-just walk slow."

Jacques looked at his lap, not wanting to meet her gaze.

"I w-walk a mile every morning on the t-treadmill b-back home. And K-kaitlynn and I have b-been walking a m-mile around the neighborhood every morning b-before we c-come to the b-beach. D-distance isn't my p-problem. Speed is."

Jacques raised his chin until he was looking at the table top.

"Jacques, for g-gosh sakes. Will you look at m-me?"

Jacques raised his head until he was looking into her eyes. She smiled her half-smile and punched him on the shoulder.

"That's b-better. I'm not mad at you. I just w-wanted you to know. You c-can make it up t-to me by b-buying me lunch."

"I didn't mean anything -" Jacques started to say.

"I know. It's okay. I'm g-glad you're here."

She put her arm around his and rested her head on his shoulder.

"Let's g-get some lunch."

The smile on Jacques' face when he walked up to the counter at Iggie's, arm in arm with Scarlett, shone bright enough to warn ships off Frying Pan Shoals on the darkest night. Warmth radiated from where her head rested on his shoulder through his whole being. They moved slowly and carefully, but steadily, to take their place in line.

The spell was broken when Kaitlynn's voice rang out from the screened-in dining room.

"Hey, Daredevil! It's about time you got here."

The scorn her voice carried the first time she called him that was gone, replaced by something closely resembling friendliness. When Jacques looked at her, she was smiling at him, a genuine smile. Trish and Marissa were smiling, too.

They must have just finished their lunch, as all that remained were three crumpled bags on the table they'd claimed. Kaitlynn got up and walked over to where Jacques and Scarlett waited in line.

"Can I count on you to get her back to our spot on the beach in one piece, Daredevil?" Kaitlynn asked, staring Jacques in the eye.

She tried to keep her tone stern, but couldn't keep the smile from her lips or twinkle out of her eyes. Unlike Scarlett's, Kaitlynn's eyes were a silver-blue. Right then, they sparkled with her smile. Jacques knew they could turn hard and cold.

"Really, Kaitlynn?" Scarlett said. "Really?"

"I'm just looking out for my baby sister," Kaitlynn said with all sincerity. "So Jacques, can I count on you?"

There was more to the question than just wanting to know if Jacques could get Scarlett back to a certain spot on beach after lunch.

"You can count on me," Jacques said, his tone serious.

"Good."

She turned and practically bounced over to where Trish and Marissa were waiting.

"Then I'll see you on the beach."

Jacques and Scarlett ordered their lunches and Jacques carried their tray to the screened in dining room. He was having a shrimp burger and onion rings. Instead of a milkshake, he'd ordered a diet Coke.

"I was thinking of g-getting a shrimp b-burger," Scarlett said as she unwrapped her chicken burger with bacon and cheese. "B-but I've never had one. I wasn't sure I'd-if I'd like it."

"Here," Jacques said, tearing off a piece of his and holding it out to her, "try a bite of mine. If you like shrimp, you're gonna love it."

Scarlett's nose twitched, reminding Jacques of a rabbit, an observation he kept to himself.

"Okay," she said. "Just a small b-bite."

She reached out and took the piece Jacques was holding, letting her fingers linger against his for a moment longer than necessary to get a good grip. Jacques' lips curled into a grin.

Scarlett slowly drew back her hand and popped the bit of shrimp burger into her mouth.

"Mmm, this is g-good. Now I wish I'd ordered one."

The look of disappointment on her face gave Jacques' heart a tug. "We can switch if you want. I like chicken burgers, too." Scarlett smiled her half-smile.

"No, th-that's okay, really. Maybe I'll g-get one t-tomorrow."

They didn't say much as they finished off their sandwiches and onion rings. It was a comfortable silence, interspersed with smiling glances and shy looks.

When they finished, Jacques stuffed the wrappers and Scarlett's bag into his and carried them to the trash can. He returned to his seat so they could finish their sodas.

Scarlett set her cup down and, with a serious look on her face said, "Jacques, c-can I ask you something?"

Jacques flicked the top of his straw a couple of times before he met her gaze. "Sure, anything."

Scarlett bit her lip. Jacques waited patiently, resisting the urge to take a sip of his drink.

Scarlett stared at the table top. When she looked up, she said, "Jacques, why did y-you want t-to have lunch with me t-today?"

Jacques almost knocked over his cup. He managed to keep it from falling over, but squeezed it so hard some ice pushed over the top and fell on the table. Pulling several napkins from the dispenser, Jacques cleaned them up before answering Scarlett's question.

"I wanted to have lunch with you because…I like you. I…when we first met yesterday…I…." Jacques took a deep breath.

"Okay, this is gonna sound corny. Yesterday when I first saw you, and looked in your eyes, I felt something. Right away, I knew I wanted to get to know you. When you came to The Bean this morning, I felt a flutter inside."

He stopped and pressed his lips tight together. Scarlett was leaning toward him, listening, her gray-green eyes wide open, her lips slightly parted, expectant.

Jacques continued. "I don't know how to explain it. Like I said, I like you and want to get to know you."

Scarlett licked her lips. Watching her do that made Jacques blood race.

"You explained it p-pretty g-good," she said, sounding breathless. "I'd s-say you explained it p-pretty good."

Jacques had kissed girls before. Well, a girl. Melanie Perkins in eighth grade, in the fiction stacks of the school library, on a dare, but he'd never kissed a girl he liked before. That didn't stop him. He leaned toward Scarlett and pressed his lips against hers.

Scarlett responded by leaning further toward him. They kind of moved their lips around some, keeping them firmly closed, until Jacques' hand struck that darned drink cup, sending ice and watery remnants of diet Coke across the table.

Scarlett stood straight up and dropped into her seat, almost falling over backward. Jacques reached out and caught her wind milling arm, keeping her upright and on the bench. In doing so, he leaned his waist against the table, his shorts absorbing the watery diet Coke running off the table there, staining them a light brown right at the crotch.

Jacques shook his head in resignation.

"Great. Just great."

Scarlett, a blush coloring her cheeks said, "It was g-great, Jacques. It was my first k-kiss, and it was g-great. I'll remember it forever."

Jacques forgot all about his wet shorts with their embarrassing stain. He reached across the table, ignoring the spilled soda and ice, and took Scarlett's hand.

"It was a great kiss," he said. "Does this mean we're boyfriend and girlfriend?"

Scarlett's blush deepened. "If you want t-to b-be. I've never had a b-boyfriend before."

Jacques squeezed her hand. "I want to be. I've never had a girlfriend before, either. That's kind of cool isn't it? We're the first for each other. That's kind of special."

Scarlett squeezed back. "You're k-kind of special."

They sat staring into each other's eyes until the cold seeping through his shorts made Jacques squirm in his seat.

"If you'll give me minute, I'm gonna clean up this mess. Then I'll run into the bathroom and change into my bathing suit. I'll be right back."

Scarlett blew him a kiss. "D-don't make me wait t-too long."

It didn't take Jacques long. After he'd cleaned the spilled soda off the table, he grabbed his bathing suit out of the saddle bag on his beach cruiser and ignored the "NO CHANGING IN THE RESTROOM" sign Iggie'd hung on the door.

That's just for tourists. Iggie doesn't care if I change in there.

Fortunately, Jacques was right about that.

When they walked out of Iggie's, Jacques realized he had a dilemma.

"What are you going to do about your bike?" Scarlett asked.

Jacques scratched his head and looked at his bike. "Wait here a minute," he said to Scarlett before running back into Iggie's.

He returned a moment later wearing a smile.

"Iggie says I can leave it locked up here and pick it up later."

Bike problem solved, Jacques and Scarlett were ready to head up the beach to meet Kaitlynn and the other girls.

"Do you want to take the sidewalk or walk on the beach?" Jacques asked.

"The beach," Scarlett said. "Down near the water."

Jacques took her hand and, slowly, they walked down to the water's edge and up the beach toward the pier.

They were almost to the pier when Scarlett spotted Kaitlynn walking toward them. Seeing their hands entwined, Kaitlynn gave Scarlett an inquisitive look.

Without waiting for an explanation Kaitlynn said, "I wasn't coming to look for you or anything. I just felt like taking a walk down the beach, maybe check out the life guards."

"I could introduce you if you want," Jacques said. "I know most of them."

Kaitlynn laughed and shook her head. "I don't want to meet them, Daredevil. They're just eye candy."

Gesturing with a nod of her head toward their clasped hands, she said, "So what's with you two, holding hands and all?"

"Jacques's my b-boyfriend now," Scarlett said.

The pride in her voice when she announced it to Kaitlynn made Jacques feel like his heart was swelling.

"He c-can hold my hand if he wants t-to."

Kaitlynn stifled a laugh. "When did all this happen? Just now, today at lunch?"

"Yes, t-today at lunch, Miss Nosy. Right after we k-kissed."

Kaitlynn didn't laugh, and Jacques felt a cold dread fill his stomach. Kaitlynn might think holding hands was cute, but kissing was another matter. Kaitlynn stood up straight and narrowed her eyes at Jacques.

"I think Daredevil and I need to have a talk."

Scarlett bristled. "No you d-don't, K-kaitlynn. And stop c-calling him that. His n-name's Jacques."

"Yes Scar. We do," Kaitlynn said through clenched teeth. "Jacques, why don't you and me go for a walk? Scarlett, you go sit with Trish and Marissa."

"You c-can't t-tell me what t-to do, K-kait."

"Yes I can, Scar. If I have to, we can call Mom and get her to decide."

Scarlett swallowed whatever comeback had been on the tip of her tongue. "Fine, b-but if you m-mess this up for m-me, I'll h-hate you forever."

Jacques stood still as a statue during their exchange. When Scarlett trudged off toward the blanket where

Trish and Marissa were sitting, he started to shake a little. Kaitlynn pointed to an empty spot of beach close to the dune separating the beach from the road.

"We can sit over there and talk, Jacques."

She pronounced his name like it referenced something unpleasant a cat might hide in the sand.

Silently, he followed her to the spot she'd pointed out. When they got there she pointed to the sand. "Sit."

Jacques sat. His nervousness was giving way to anger, but he bit his tongue.

Kaitlynn sat down next to him. "You want to tell me what kind of game you're playing with my sister?"

"I'm not playing any stupid games, Kait."

Jacques knew he wasn't keeping his anger in check. He'd said her name the same way she'd just said his. Her eyes flew open wide.

"I really like Scarlett. Sorry if you have a problem with that, but it's your problem, not hers, not mine!"

Kaitlynn's jaw dropped. She closed her mouth and swallowed hard a couple of times. Guilt she'd anticipated. A hasty apology and a promise to leave Scarlett alone, she'd planned on. An angry affirmation of his affection for her sister? That took Kaitlynn by surprise.

"You're serious," she said. "You honestly like her. I mean like a boyfriend like her?"

"God, what kind of a sister are you?"

Jacques' temper was up, and his words cut deep. "You don't think a guy could like Scarlett? Why? Because she's not as pretty as you? Well, guess what? I think she is. She's got a beauty that doesn't stop at the surface. Scarlett's pretty inside and out."

The inference that Scarlett was and Kaitlynn wasn't lay there on the sand between Scarlett's boyfriend and her sister.

When the tears welled up in Kaitlynn's eyes, it was Jacques turn to be surprised. Shame began to replace his anger. He'd wanted to make Kaitlynn cry, but his success gave him no satisfaction.

"You don't know anything about Scarlett or me," Kaitlynn said.

Her words came out in a hiss. Tears rolled down her cheeks.

"You have no idea what she's been through since the accident, what I've done to keep her from getting hurt. You haven't stayed up crying with her all night about things people have said about her looks, the way she walks, and the way she talks. You have no idea."

Kaitlynn turned her back on Jacques. Her shoulders shook with sobs.

Jacques sat there at a loss for what to do. He gathered his courage, and his humility, reached out a shaking hand, and touched Kaitlynn's shoulder. She tensed, but didn't pull away.

"I'm sorry," he said as gently as he could. "You're right. I have no idea about those things, but I care about Scarlett, a lot. So why don't you tell me. I'm not going to hurt her, Kaitlynn. I promise."

Jacques's gentle, sincere tone reached through Kaitlynn's anger and fear. She'd feared he was another guy out to make a fool out of Scarlett by building her up and then shooting her down. When she turned and saw the genuine concern in his soft, brown eyes, the hint of tears forming there, she believed him.

"Five years ago, when Scarlett was ten, I was fifteen. We were going with my aunt to the mall. I had my learner's permit, so my aunt let me drive. We were almost there. I'd just stopped behind a couple of other cars at a red light."

Kaitlynn stopped. Telling about the day of the accident was always hard.

"Scarlett dropped her purse on the floor. Before me or my aunt could stop her, she'd unbuckled her seat belt and reached down to get it.

"She'd almost got buckled back up when the SUV hit us. The cops said the woman driving never even slowed down. Dead drunk at two in the afternoon, she never even saw us sitting there.

"The SUV pushed us into the car ahead of us. Both ends of my aunt's Accord were smashed, but we would have been all right, or mostly all right.

"I got some whiplash. The airbag saved me. The other one saved my aunt. There wasn't an airbag in the back.

"Scarlett would have been okay if she'd gotten her seatbelt back on. Instead, she got thrown around like a ragdoll."

Kaitlynn told Jacques all this with her eyes focused on the sand. Tears rolled down her cheeks. She turned and looked at Jacques.

"I know it wasn't my fault. We were just sitting there."

She took a deep breath, looked down at the sand again, and continued.

"Scarlett's face hit the edge of the front passenger seat. That's what caused the scar and smashed her nose. She actually lost part of her nose. That happened when we hit the car in front of us. She broke her back and hip when the SUV first hit. That's why she walks like she does.

"The doctors aren't sure which hit on the head caused the stuttering. She didn't stutter before the accident." Kaitlynn sighed.

"So now you know. They did everything they could for her. The lady that hit us had great insurance. Her husband was loaded."

"Now I know what happened," Jacques said, his voice a hoarse whisper. He cleared his throat. "And I can only imagine what she's been through since. I know how mean kids can be. I see it all the time in school."

Kaitlynn shook her head. "You think you can imagine, but it was worse. I can't count the days she came home crying, but as she got older, she learned to deal with it. And she did pretty well, until Kenny."

Jacques didn't know Kenny, but he immediately despised him. "Kenny broke her heart?"

"He asked her to the big end of year dance in the eighth grade, and then when she showed up at the dance he told everyone she was making it up and he'd never asked her."

Jacques felt anger surge through him. "If I ever meet Kenny, it'll be his funeral."

Kaitlynn's smile chilled Jacques. "I already took care of Kenny. And don't ask, because I ain't telling. Let's just say he'll regret what he did whenever he…never mind."

Jacques laughed and Kaitlynn joined him.

"So, you really like my annoying little sister?"

"Yes," Jacques said. "I really like your little sister."

"Okay. I guess I can let you live."

Jacques snorted. "I'm glad. I'm kind of fond of living."

Kaitlynn rose gracefully from the sand, turned, and reached out to help Jacques to his feet. Jacques took her hand and his eyes strayed from her face to her black bikini top, for just a second, before snapping back to Kaitlynn's silver-blue eyes. The look of tolerant amusement on her face let Jacques know she'd noticed where he'd glanced.

Heat colored Jacques cheeks as he rose to stand beside Kaitlynn.

"Uh, sorry, couldn't help it. They were right there."

Kaitlynn's jaw dropped. The blush on Jacques face darkened.

"Oh, God. I'm sorry. That didn't come out right."

Kaitlynn smiled and patted his shoulder. "It's okay," she said. "Just make sure you give Scarlett the same attention."

Then, realizing what she'd just said, Kaitlynn tried to recover. "I can't believe I just said that. What I meant was -"

Kaitlynn stopped when she saw the shocked look on Jacques' face, and then started laughing. Jacques' stunned look was replaced by confusion and finally, he laughed along with her.

When she managed to stop laughing Kaitlynn said, "We'd better get over to Scarlett. She's going to think I ran you off."

Scarlett was sitting on the blanket with her arms around her knees, staring out at the ocean. They could see where tracks of tears had dried on her cheeks.

"Scarlett," Kaitlynn said softly as they approach. "Look who survived my third degree."

Scarlett's pouting lips twitched, but she didn't lift her head.

"Maybe she was hoping you'd scared me off," Jacques said.

Scarlett's head popped up and she focused her gaze on Jacques like a laser beam. She tried to keep her angry expression, but it didn't work. The fact that he was there, that Kaitlynn hadn't scared him off, brightened her heart and she couldn't hide how happy it made her.

"I w-was afraid you wouldn't c come back. I thought I might n-not see you again," Scarlett said as she struggled to stand.

Jacques and Kaitlynn both reached down to help her up, bumping heads in the process.

With a loud, "Ouch," they both recoiled and rubbed their heads. Scarlett failed to suppress a chuckle. Her boyfriend and her sister glared at her.

Then Kaitlynn said to Jacques, "You're her boyfriend; you help her up."

"What's this about a boyfriend?" Trish asked. She and Marissa saw the three of them gathered at the blanket and came out of the surf to see what was up.

Kaitlynn held her hands out towards Jacques. "Daredevil here has swept my little sister off her feet. Now he's trying to help her stand up."

Scarlett got to her feet with Jacques's help, and glared at Kaitlynn. "I t-told you not to c-call him that."

Kaitlynn raised her hands in surrender. "Okay, okay. I give."

She turned to meet Trish and Marissa's expectant gazes.

"Jacques and Scarlett are an item."

Marissa lowered her chin and looked at Jacques and Scarlett through incredibly long lashes just as blond as her hair, and said, "Really? You don't waste any time, do you island boy?"

Her words might have stung if not for the smile that lit her whole face, from her violet hued blue eyes to her perfectly straight, bright white teeth.

Trish was a little more reserved.

"I hope it works out. Long distance relationships can be tough."

Jacques brow furrowed. "It won't be that long distance. Y'all just live over on the mainland, right?"

He looked at Scarlett, who was studying her toes, and then at Kaitlynn. "Right?"

"Trish, Marissa, and I share a house in Myrtle Grove. Scarlett's visiting with us for a couple of weeks."

Kaitlynn grimaced. "Then she has to go home to Canton."

Jacques felt a cold chill sweep over him. "I thought you lived nearby. I guess I should have asked. I should have known."

The light touch of Scarlett's fingertips on his chin encouraged him to turn and meet her eyes.

"I'm sorry I didn't t-tell you. I n-never thought about it. Meeting you, and having y-you like me, I forgot all about h-having to ever go home."

Losing himself once again in her beautiful eyes, Jacques decided he didn't care if they only had the rest of the day, the rest of the week, or the rest of their lives, he was going to enjoy every minute they could spend together.

Jacques reached up and pressed Scarlett's hand against his cheek. "Long distance isn't what is used to be," he said. "With Facebook and Twitter and texting, we can still talk every day. And we've got two weeks. It's more than some people get."

Scarlett's lips quivered. She moved against Jacques and rested her head on his chest. His arms went around her and pulled her tight. Scarlett wrapped her arms around him and held on like she never wanted to let go.

"Okay, you two," Kaitlynn said. "You're on the beach after all. Do we need to toss you in the ocean to cool you off?"

Jacques felt Scarlett start to shake as she laughed. "No, K-kait. We don't need a d-dunking."

She lifted her face to Jacques. "B-but I would like to g-get my feet wet. Come with me?"

"Okay," Jacques said.

Hand in hand they made their way through the throng of beach goers to the water's edge.

Spending the whole afternoon at the beach could have had disastrous consequences for Jacques if Scarlett hadn't been more than adequately supplied with sun block. The best part of the afternoon, in Jacques opinion, was applying the sun block to each other's backs. In a way, it was also the most disturbing, because the scars from the surgery that repaired Scarlett's spine were visible just above the lower part of the open back of her shimmering blue, one-piece bathing suit.

CHAPTER NINE

On Sunday mornings The Parisian Bean didn't open until seven. It was Marie's one concession to the weekend, getting an extra hour of sleep on Sunday morning.

"So why am I lying here looking at my stupid alarm clock at four-thirty wishing I was still asleep?" Jacques said to the glowing digits on his clock/radio.

He rolled onto his back and stared at his ceiling. Nature gave him a call, and Jacques knew he wouldn't be getting back to sleep.

With his eyes opened only enough to keep him from running into the door, Jacques navigated from his room to the bathroom next door. On the third try, his tired hand found the light switch. He squinted hard against the glare that burned into his brain. "Stupid light."

Once Jacques' eyes adjusted, he answered nature's call, washed his hands, and looked at himself in the mirror. He looked blurry.

"Stupid glasses."

Jacques gave a disgusted sigh, turned out the light on his way out the door, and went back to his room. His glasses were right where he'd left them, on his nightstand. The digits on his clock showed 4:35.

Jacques gnawed on his lower lip and looked around the room.

"It's too early to go downstairs," he told the clock. "Mr. Bagley knows we don't open til seven on Sunday so he won't even show up until six-thirty." The clock responded by changing to 4:36.

Jacques ran his hand over his head and said, "Yeah, that's what I thought you'd say."

Walking over to the window, Jacques turned the handle to open the slats on the blind. The slats appeared to be white painted wood, but were really some kind of plastic. Marie had told him they'd last longer than wood and be easier to clean. Jacques hadn't really cared, as long as they kept it dark when he was trying to sleep.

Outside everything had a sheen to it, and Jacques noticed a fine drizzle falling through the dim light of the street lamp near the front door of the café. He heaved a sigh and shook his head.

To the street lamp, he said, "Great. If it's raining, I wonder if Kaitlynn will even bring Scarlett to the beach?"

Behind him the clock changed to 4:37.

Jacques shrugged. Leaving the blinds open, he moved the couple of steps to his desk, opened the lid on his laptop, and punched the button to turn on the twenty-one inch screen attached to it. He ran two screens at the same time. What he was working on would be on the big screen. He kept his Facebook page and e-mail program open on the laptop screen where he could check them without disturbing whatever was on the big screen.

Since he had nothing he was working on, Jacques pulled his Facebook page up on the big screen. He had a friend request from Kaitlynn. It showed they had one mutual friend.

"I don't have to look to see who that is," Jacques said to the computer screen.

He moved the cursor to Confirm and clicked. Clicking on the globe icon to see what the two notifications waiting to be read were, he was pleased to see Ginger had accepted his friend request. He'd searched for her before going to bed, after chatting on-line with Scarlett right up until his curfew. Ginger wasn't hard to find on Facebook. She was the only "Ginger Mumples" listed when he searched.

Behind him, the clock changed to 4:38.

Next to the Notifications icon, the Message icon showed Jacques had one message unread. "I wonder who that's from?" he asked the screen.

One click later, he knew.

Jacques, you probably don't remember me, but we share a last name. My first name is Sean. I'm your father. I understand if you don't want to hear from me, but I hope you'll give me a chance.

I'm not the man I was when I left you and your mother. I'd like to get to know you. If you're willing to give me that chance, message back.
Sean

Behind him, the clock changed to 4:39.

Jacques stared at the message on the screen. He wasn't angry, or sad, or glad. He was numb.

Sean O'Larrity wasn't a real person to Jacques. He was a ghost, someone who existed once, a long time ago, but disappeared. Jacques hardly remembered him. He never expected to hear from him. He certainly never expected to get a message from his absentee father on his Facebook page.

"I wonder if it's even really him."

The computer didn't answer. It just sat there showing the message on the screen.

"I oughta just delete it. It's probably not even really him. Even if it is, what do I care?" But he did care. If it was really his father, Jacques did care. His temper began to build.

"I oughta message him back and tell him to go to hell. I don't want to get to know him. I know all I need to know about him. He's a bum and a creep and a loser and an -"

"Jacques, what in the world are you yelling about?" Marie said as she flung open his door. "I heard you yelling and thought you were having a nightmare."

He stopped his rant mid-word when his mother burst in the room. His breath heaved in and out of his lungs. He couldn't form the words to tell her what was on his computer screen, so he pointed at it.

Marie walked slowly toward his desk.

"Okay, JQ. I'll take a look. Why don't you put some pants on?"

Jacques glanced down. He was wearing nothing but the boxers he slept in. Relief flooded him when he saw the fly was buttoned. Grabbing a pair of cargo shorts from his chest-of-drawers, he hastily pulled them on.

While he was finding a pair of shorts, Marie read the message from someone claiming to be her estranged husband. She hadn't heard from him since the day, when Jacques was three, that Sean left their apartment in a drunken rage, swearing never to return. He never had and she'd never looked for him.

Jacques moved up to stand beside her.

"It might not even be him. I was trying to decide whether to delete it or cuss him out."

Marie sighed and slid her arm around his shoulders. "You'll do neither. Let me answer for you."

She sat down at Jacques' desk and keyed in a reply.

Sean. This is Marie. If that's really you, you've got a lot of nerve. What? Are you drunk again? Still? You promised you'd never return. So keep your promise. Jacques and I don't need you or your baggage.

She looked up at Jacques. "How's that?"

Jacques lips curled into a wry smile. "Just right."

Marie hit Send.

"Since we're up," Marie said, "why don't I make us some breakfast?"

"Pancakes and sausage?"

Marie rubbed his head.

"I'll see what we've got. It may be Cheerios and milk."

A few minutes later they were seated at the kitchen table, bowls of Cheerios and milk before them, mugs of steaming hot, fresh brewed coffee in their hands.

"You know, JQ, I should probably go shopping sometime. There's nothing in this apartment to eat."

"It's okay, Mom. We never eat here anyway."

He meant to be reassuring, but his words stung Marie.

"I know we don't, honey, and I'm sorry about that. I'm your mom. I should cook you a decent meal once in a while."

Jacques set his mug down and put his hand on hers.

"You make dinner for me every night during the school year. You're always here when I come home. So I've gone a couple of days without a home cooked meal. We went out for pizza Friday night, and last night we had sandwiches at The Cone, giving business to our new neighbors."

He smiled and shrugged. "It's not like it's a trend, Mom."

Marie reached out with her other hand and brushed his bangs out of his eyes. "You've got your father's eyes, you know. I'd almost forgotten that."

Jacques sat up straight. "I hope that's all I got from him."

Marie took a deep breath. "Your father wasn't all bad, Jacques. After all, I fell in love with him. It wasn't until...."

"It wasn't until what, Mom?" Jacques asked.

"It wasn't until the drinking got out of control," Marie said. "It changed him. He got where he was drunk all the time. Then your grandfather cut him out of the will and left everything to you."

"That's why he left, Mom? He was mad at Grandpa Pat?"

Marie stared into her coffee mug. Jacques thought she wasn't going to say anything more. Marie picked up the mug, stood, walked over to the coffee maker on the counter, and poured herself a refill. She held the carafe up to Jacques, silently asking him if he wanted more. He shook his head. She replaced the carafe on the warmer and returned to her seat.

"The will was just the last straw. Your father and your grandpa Pat hadn't been on good terms for a couple of years. Not from the time Sean started drinking again." She paused to take another sip of coffee.

"What I didn't know, JQ, was that your father'd gotten in trouble with booze when he was still in high school. No one told me when we started dating. They didn't tell me when we got engaged, or when we got married. Sean was sober all that time... at least when he was around me. I didn't find out about his early bouts with alcoholism until after he left."

Jacques tried to digest what he was learning about the father he never knew. Over the years, he'd picked up that Sean had been a drunk. At one time, his father'd been a fixture in The Sand Bar, but then he'd walked out on them and disappeared from their lives. Now he wanted back in.

"Why do you think my father decided to contact me now, after all this time?"

Marie shook her head. "There's no telling." She looked Jacques hard in the eye. "Do you want to see him?"

"No. I don't think so. I just wonder, why now?"

"You could message him on the computer and ask him," Marie said.

Glancing at the clock on the coffee maker she noticed it was time to head down to the shop.

"Why don't you come down later, after you've had some time to consider all this. I can handle things this morning. It's Sunday, and it's raining. Likely to be a slow morning."

Jacques finished his soggy Cheerios. Before heading back to his room, he washed the bowls and mugs and put them back in the cabinet.

When he got to his room, he noticed a chat box had opened on Facebook. Next to a picture of Tara, from "Gone with the Wind," was the question,

what r u doin up so early, followed by, **no answer, huh. maybe you fell asleep still logged in.**

"What in the world is Scarlett doing up so early?" Jacques asked the computer.

He sat down and typed,

was having brkfst with mom. just got ur msg. what r u doin up this early?

Jacques knew Scarlett was still logged in by the green light next to her name on the chat list, but he didn't know if she was at her computer. The proof that she was came in seconds.

t-storm woke me up. is it rainin @ beach?

Jacques remembered the rain, but couldn't recall hearing any thunder. "That could have been what woke me up."

drizzling here right now. think maybe t-storm woke me 2. will u come 2 beach if rainin?

Scarlett didn't reply right away. Jacques shivered sitting there in just shorts. The storm brought a cold front with it. He got up and changed into jeans and a UNCW t-shirt. When he sat back down, he saw Scarlett had answered.

sorry. K woke up and asked me what I'm doin. told her I was flirting w/u on fb. she mumbled something and went back to sleep. don't think we'll go 2 beach 2day. T&M want 2 go mall. K says we'll go aft church.

oh. then won't c u 2day I guess. bummer.

I kno. want 2 c u 2. miss u.

miss u 2. gotta go 2 work. ttyl.

c u. xo.

xo.

Jacques smiled. He and Scarlett had virtually hugged and kissed each other.

"I'd rather really hug and kiss her."

Every rainy morning, Jacques wished there was a way to go right from the apartment to The Bean without going outside. "Stupid rain."

He ran from the doorway at the bottom of the stairs, around Buzby Beach Bikes, until he got to the awning over FITU2A-T. From there he was mostly sheltered from the rain.

It was just after six-thirty when he walked into The Bean. Mr. Bagley waved at him as he drove off in the Buzby Bakery Truck.

"Does he ever take a day off?" Jacques asked the back of the truck as it disappeared into the gloom.

A low rumble that didn't come from the truck answered him. Jacques looked up and noticed the raindrops were getting bigger and coming down harder. A gust of wind blew some his way.

"Stupid wind," Jacques said wiping at the drops on his jeans.

He was about to open the door into the café when he noticed someone seated at the table by the window.

"We're not open yet. I wonder who that is."

Condensation from the damp air, and the rain now blowing in, made the window hard to see through. Jacques pushed open the door. When the bells jangled, the early customer turned to see who was coming in.

Jacques' glasses were spotted with rain. He took them off and wiped them with the tail of his t-shirt. Slipping them back on, he took a good look at the customer, who was still looking at him.

"Morning, Jacques," the customer said.

His eyes widening in surprise, Jacques recognized Scout. And at the same time, he didn't. Gone was the shaggy hair and scraggly beard. The sleeveless denim shirt had been replaced with a golf shirt sporting the Buzby Pier logo. In place of Scout's ragged cut-offs, he wore a neat pair of khaki cargo shorts. An apparently new pair of deck shoes covered his feet.

"Good morning Scout," Jacques said a moment too late, after he realized he was staring. "Sorry, I almost didn't recognize you at first."

"Not surprised. Got a haircut."

Scout's haircut hadn't done much to make him more talkative. "It looks good. Need a refill on your coffee?"

Scout shook his head. "I'm good. Thought you opened at six."

"We usually do, but things are usually slow on Sunday, so Mom opens at seven."

"I'll remember," Scout said.

He returned to his seat, picked up his cup, and returned to watching the rain.

Jacques stared at him for a few seconds more before going behind the counter. Marie was in the kitchen, having already sorted the bakery delivery. Jacques knocked on the door frame.

Marie wiped her hands on her apron, walked over, and gave him a hug.

"How ya doing, JQ? Up to working today."

"I'm fine, Mom. Really. I'm not gonna let it bother me." Jacques changed the subject.

"I wonder what's up with Scout. The haircut, new clothes. I guess he got tired of looking like a hermit, huh?"

"I think he looks very nice. He told me he's got a job at the pier. Kid they had working the bait counter up and quit. Scout was right there. Mr. Kelsey offered him the job on the spot, and Scout took it."

"Where'd you hear all that?" Jacques asked.

"Scout told me this morning when I asked him what was new." She glanced at the cat-tail clock over the ovens.

"You'd better get out front and get ready to open up. It's almost seven."

Jacques kissed his mom on the cheek, and then went out to turn the sign around. He'd just started mixing his Buzby Bucket of caramel macchiato when Scout turned to him and said, "Customer."

By the time Scout turned back to the window, the door opened and Cienna walked in, shaking the rain off her windbreaker.

"Hi, Jacques."

She looked over at Scout, but he was looking out the window. She moved up to the counter.

"Hey, Cienna. Is your grandma coming?"

"Nah," Cienna said. "She and grandpa said since it was raining, and since I was up, it'd be really nice of me to come over and get their coffee."

Jacques chuckled. He could picture Mrs. Philbert doing that.

"It's not funny, JQ. That wind made a mess of my hair, just crossing the street."

Jacques was about to tell her that he thought her hair looked fine when a deep rumble shook the windows and the lights flickered.

"Oh, no. Please. Not that. Let the power stay on."

Marie came out from the kitchen. "Did the lights just blink out here?"

Jacques glanced at the cash register and noticed the little clock in the corner of the screen was blinking all zeros. He heaved a sigh.

"Yup, and it made the register reboot."

"Well let's hope all it does is blink," Marie said. "We won't be able to do much business if it goes out altogether."

"Need a generator," Scout said.

Jacques jumped. He hadn't noticed Scout leave his seat and walk to the counter. "Wouldn't have to worry about the storm."

"I know," Marie said. "I've thought of that before. Problem is where to put it."

Scout's lips twisted, and he nodded his head. He handed Marie his empty coffee mug. "Thanks for the coffee."

The first smile Jacques had ever seen on his face curled Scout's lips.

Marie took the mug. "Anytime, Scout."

"Gotta go to work. See you tomorrow."

"Okay," Marie said. "I'll see you then."

Scout nodded to her once, turned on his heel, and went out into the rain.

"He's gonna get soaked," Cienna said. "Where does he work anyway?"

Marie watched Scout through the door. She saw him pull a poncho out of his cargo pants pocket and put it on.

She smiled. "He'll be okay." She turned to Cienna. "He got a job at the pier."

Then she headed back to the kitchen, saying as she went, "I hope the power holds out long enough for me to fill those orders."

Cienna looked at the puzzled expression on Jacques' face. "What?"

Jacques shook his head. "I don't know. Did it seem to you there was something with my mom and Scout?"

Cienna started to tell Jacques he was crazy, but something about the way Marie watched Scout until he'd put the poncho on stuck with her. "I don't know. How old's your mom?"

Jacques closed his eyes and bit his lip. "Let's see, last birthday she was...I'm fifteen and she had me when she was twenty, no twenty-one, so, thirty-six. She's thirty-six."

Cienna pursed her lips. "I see. And how old do you think Scout is?"

Jacques shrugged. "I don't know. He's kind-of old. He might be as old as my mom."

"Scout and your mom. That would explain the haircut and new shoes," Cienna said.

Jacques frowned. "I'm not sure if I like the idea of Scout and my mom. My mom already has a boyfriend, sort of, Mr. Warren. They go out sometimes."

"That doesn't sound like much of a romance, Jacques."

"Well how romantic could Scout be? I mean, c'mon, Cienna. He's pretty much a bum."

Cienna's eyes narrowed and she slapped Jacques on the shoulder. "That's pretty harsh."

She got a starry look in her eyes. "I think he's more of the mysterious recluse, a prisoner to memories he can't suppress until he meets the beautiful maiden who can release him from his painful past."

Jacques snorted and shook his head. "You need to stay out of the romance book section of your grandparent's store."

"You wouldn't know romance if it bit you on the butt," Cienna said.

Jacques retort was cut short by Cienna's phone playing "Over the River and Through the Woods."

"Oops," Cienna said. "That's my grandma. She's probably wondering what's taking so long."

"Really," Jacques said. "That's her ring tone? Really?"

Cienna turned her back on him, hit Talk, and put the phone to her ear.

"Hi, Grandma."

She was quiet while she listened to Mrs. Philbert.

"No, nothing's wrong. The power's on. Jacques and I were just talking."

Cienna turned and looked at Jacques. He was already getting Mr. and Mrs. Philbert's coffees ready.

"Jacques getting them ready right now. I'll be just a couple more minutes." Cienna nodded, aware that her grandmother couldn't see it.

"Yes, Grandma. I'll be careful."

Another short pause, and then Cienna said, "I love you too, Grandma," before hitting End and putting her phone back in her purse.

An ominous rumble of thunder rattled the windows and caused the lights to go out for a couple of seconds.

"Oh, great. There goes the register again," Jacques said.

Cienna laughed.

"I guess you'll have to figure out what to charge the old fashioned way."

Jacques reached under the counter and pulled out an old, four-function calculator.

"Yup," he said.

That made Cienna laugh even harder.

CHAPTER TEN

After Cienna left, the café was empty for a while. Outside the wind blew, the rain poured, and the occasional thunder continued to rattle the windows.

"At least the lights are staying on," Jacques said to Maria when she brought her freshly baked cakes out of the kitchen to cool on the decorating table.

"They can go out now if they want. That's all the cakes I have to bake."

"What about mixing the frosting?" Jacques asked.

Marie wiped her sleeve across her brow. "I can mix it by hand if I have to. Of course, it'd be a lot easier if the power does stay on and I can use the mixer."

Marie went in back to clean up the kitchen while the cakes cooled.

Jacques was wishing he'd brought his laptop down. *Then I could check Facebook and maybe chat with Scarlett.*

The wind outside gusted, rattling the door on its hinges, and splattering the rain hard against the windows. The staccato rhythm reminded Jacques of paint balls hitting a wall.

Staring through the rain, Jacques thought he was imagining things when he saw a pink Jeep pull up in front of the café. When he realized it really was Kaitlynn's Jeep, he ran to the door and held it open as Kaitlynn and Scarlett slowly made their way across the sidewalk, protected by a huge golf umbrella emblazoned with the UNCW Seahawk emblem. As soon as they crossed the threshold, Jacques pulled the door closed and put his arms around Scarlett. She rested her head on his chest and shivered. Kaitlynn closed the umbrella and started to shake it off, but stopped, opened the door a crack, and shook the water off outside. Jacques watched her until she pulled the umbrella in and closed the door.

"Thanks," he said.

"For not getting your floor all wet or for bringing Scar?" Kaitlynn said, a teasing grin on her face.

"Both," Jacques said, tightening his arms around Scarlett.

Marie came out and spotted her son embracing a young lady.

"Well, well, Jacques. What's this? Are we hugging every customer who comes in on a rainy day like this?"

Kaitlynn's eyes darted back and forth between Marie and Jacques. Scarlett stiffened in his arms, and pushed him away. Jacques rolled his eyes. He recognized the playful tone in his mother's voice.

"Mom, I'd like you to meet someone."

He took Scarlett's hand and led her to where Marie was standing by the end of the counter. "Scarlett, this is my mom, Marie O'Larrity. Mom, this is Scarlett Henderson, my girlfriend. The other young lady is Kaitlynn, Scarlett's sister."

Marie offered her hand to Scarlett. "So you're the lovely young lady who's stolen my son's heart. I feel like I already know you. You're all he talked about at dinner last night."

Jacques started to object, but stopped when he saw the smile on Scarlett's face and sensed the way she relaxed at Marie's friendly manner. In truth, all he'd told his mother during their quick dinner of sandwiches next door at The Beach Cone was that he'd spent the afternoon at the beach with his new friend Scarlett and her sister. The rest of the time they talked to the Mumples about how their first day had gone.

"Jacques t-told me a lot about you t-too, Mrs. O'Larrity. I'm g-glad to get t-to meet you."

Marie looked from Scarlett to Kaitlynn. "You two must be freezing. Jacques will fix you up something hot to drink. What would you like?"

"I'll take a Bucket of White Chocolate Mocha," Kaitlynn said. "And maybe one of those croissants in the case there. Those things are huge. Scarlett, want to split one with me?"

"Sure," Scarlett said. "Jacques, I'd just like a b-big hot chocolate, b-but not a whole b-bucket."

"I'm on it," Jacques said.

Then on impulse, he kissed Scarlett's cheek. Marie's eyes went wide, but she held her tongue. Kaitlynn was looking at the pastry display and missed it. Scarlett's eyes sparkled and her smile warmed Jacques' heart. He practically skipped behind the counter to make their drinks.

Scarlett and Kaitlynn sat at the same table Scout used earlier in the morning. Jacques brought their drinks and waited until they'd tried them before heading back to the counter to get their croissant.

Marie met him at the counter, handed him the croissant – which she'd cut in two and put on separate plates – and his Bucket of caramel macchiato.

"Why don't you go sit with your friends? I can manage the rest of this crowd." She smiled and gestured around the empty café.

Jacques returned her smile. "Thanks, Mom."

He set the girls' croissant before them and pulled up a chair. Thunder rumbled overhead, rattling the windows, and they all looked out at the storm.

"I was surprised to see y'all pull up," Jacques said. "What made you decide to drive all the way out here in this storm?"

A bashful smile formed on Scarlett's face and she turned away from Jacques. Kaitlynn set her Bucket down.

"If you're not gonna tell him, I will."

She didn't wait for Scarlett to respond before launching into the story.

"Scar was moping around the house, moaning about how she wasn't going to get to go to the beach today because of the storm."

Scarlett looked at Jacques out of the corner of her eye, but said nothing. Kaitlynn shook her head.

"I don't know who she thought she was kidding. The beach. Really, Scar? I know why you were bumming."

Jacques was trying hard to keep a silly grin off his face. He reached out and put his hand on Scarlett's.

Continuing her story, Kaitlynn said, "I couldn't stand to see her wandering around the house all gloomy, so I told her we could go out for coffee and breakfast, and here we are." Scarlett turned soft eyes on Kaitlynn.

"Thank you for b-being such a sweet, understanding sister, K-kait. You know I love you for it."

Kaitlynn pulled off a piece of her croissant.

"I know, Scar. I love you, too," she said just before popping the piece of pastry in her mouth.

Jacques opened his mouth to tell Kaitlynn how glad he was she'd brought Scarlett to the café, but his words were drowned out by a crack of thunder. The lights went out. This time they stayed out.

As the thunder subsided, from behind the cake case they heard Marie say, "Oh, great!" Then the rain, which had been coming down hard, started falling in torrents.

Jacques got up and walked over to the cake case.

"Is everything all right, Mom?"

"It will be," Marie said. "But if the lights don't come back on, I'll have to mix all this frosting by hand after all."

Jacques felt Scarlett move up to stand beside him.

"C-can I help? I'm p-pretty g-good at mixing up f-f-frosting. I help my m-mom all the t-time."

From back at the table, Kaitlynn called out, "She does. And no kidding, she is good at it." Marie put her hands behind her back, stretched, bit her lip, and eyed Scarlett.

"You sure you don't mind helping out?"

"I'd love t-to."

"Then I guess I'll have to put you on the payroll."

She pulled a flashlight from the drawer under the register and motioned to the back of the café.

"C'mon, let's find you an apron, and I'll show you what to do." Scarlett followed Marie toward the kitchen.

"You d-don't have to p-pay me. I'm g-glad to help."

"If you do as good a job as I think you'll do, it'll be worth every penny."

Jacques stood by the cake case, trying to figure out what had just happened. He turned to Kaitlynn and said, "Did my mom just hire my girlfriend?"

Kaitlynn raised her Bucket and tipped it toward him. "Just figured that out, did you?"

Jacques nodded, then shook his head, and finally shrugged. "How you doing on that Bucket? Ready for a refill?"

Kaitlynn shook the Bucket. "Nah, it's pretty full. There's a lot of coffee in one of these things."

Marie and Scarlett reappeared from the back of the store, Scarlett now wearing a dark blue Parisian Bean apron. Ignoring Jacques, they got busy at the decorating table.

Behind him, the door bells jangled. Jacques turned to see who else braved the storm in search of coffee.

Mr. Mumples, with Ginger on his heels, came in.

Mr. Mumples pushed back the hood of his rain coat. "Thought I'd come over and see if y'all were all right. Ginger and I just got into the shop when the power went out."

"Well, if you want some coffee, I've got a whole dispenser full and another pot that finished brewing just before we lost the lights," Jacques said, stepping behind the counter. "Might as well drink it before it turns cold."

"On the house," Marie called from the decorating table.

"Y'all don't have a generator?" Mr. Mumples asked.

"I've been meaning to see about getting one installed," Marie said. "But I only think about it when I need one, like today."

Mr. Mumples took the cup of coffee Jacques offered him. "Thanks, Jacques." He turned back to Marie. "I went ahead and had a backup generator installed during the remodel. It doesn't put out enough juice to run the whole store, but it will keep the fridges and freezers going. Can't afford to let all that ice cream melt."

Jacques asked Ginger if she wanted some coffee.

"No thanks," she said. "Uh, Jacques, is that Scarlett working with your mom?"

"Uh, huh," Jacques said. "And Kaitlynn's over there by the window. They came out for coffee and breakfast before heading back to church."

"Um, guys?" Kaitlynn said, holding up her cell phone. "Does anyone have a radio? A battery operated radio?"

Jacques looked at Marie. She shook her head.

"I don't think so. Not down here, anyway."

"We don't have one, do we Dad?" Ginger said.

Mr. Mumples shook his head.

Kaitlynn said, "Bummer. Trish just called and told me she heard on TV that the bridge to Buzby Island was closed. I guess Scarlett and I are going to be here a while."

"Did she say what happened to the bridge?" Mr. Mumples asked.

"No. Just that it was closed."

Thunder rumbled in the distance.

"Sounds like the storms moved out over the ocean," Mr. Mumples said.

"Dad," Ginger said, looking at her cell phone screen. "Mom's back at the house. She wants to know where we are."

"What's she doing at the house?" he asked.

"She couldn't get over the bridge. There's some kind of wreck out in the middle."

"Did you tell her we're here at the coffee shop?"

"She wants to know if we're coming home, or should she come here."

"I'd like to say we'll just go home. Things'll be pretty slow today I imagine, with this storm. But it's only our second day open, so I guess we'd better stay."

"I'll tell her," Ginger said.

Mr. Mumples raised his cup to Marie. "Thanks for the coffee, Marie. I guess me and Ginger are gonna go next door and see about getting ready to open."

"Anytime, AW," Marie said, walking with them to the door.

Jacques wanted to offer to help the Mumples, but didn't want to leave The Bean with Scarlett there. Help came from an unexpected direction.

"If you guys could use a hand," Kaitlynn said to Mr. Mumples as he reached the door, "it looks like I've got some time on my hands. Anything I can do?"

Mr. Mumples looked puzzled by her offer.

Marie told him, "This is Kaitlynn. She and Scarlett are Jacques' friends. I just put Scarlett to work helping me with the frosting."

Mr. Mumples brow furrowed as he considered Kaitylnn's offer.

Finally he shrugged and said, "Okay, I'm sure we could use your help for today."

The rain had let up considerably, and the three of them dashed out and ran next door. Scarlett walked over to the cake case as the door closed. "Where's Kait going?"

"Next door," Jacques said. "To help out the Mumples."

"You think they'll be very busy today?" Scarlett asked, leaning across the case and waggling her eyebrows at Jacques.

Jacques noticed it was only her right brow that waggled. He figured the scar through the left one kept it from moving much. Instead of accentuating the scar, though, it gave the gesture a quirky cuteness that made Jacques smile.

"What are you smiling at?" Scarlett asked.

"At how cute you are," Jacques said, surprising himself as much as Scarlett.

Her cheeks turned an adorable shade of deep pink. "Thank you, JQ. I think you're pretty cute, too."

Marie cleared her throat with theatric exaggeration. "Now that we've established how cute the two of you are, can we get back to work?"

Jacques and Scarlett turned quickly from each other. "Yes, ma'am," they chorused.

Marie felt a little stab of guilt at having embarrassed them. They were cute, the way they looked at each other and talked to each other, but her protective Mom gene was kicking in, too.

Marie was used to Jacques having friends who were girls; girls he knew from school and around the island. He and Cienna spent her two weeks at the Philbert's every summer practically joined at the hip. Girl friends, per se, didn't bother her. It was the idea of a girlfriend that triggered her Mom radar.

It wasn't because Marie didn't like Scarlett. Marie found Scarlett to be smart, polite, and pretty good company at the decorating table.

Scarlett's a pretty, young lady, Marie thought. *Her scars are noticeable, but they hardly detract from her attractiveness.*

But Scarlett is summer people, and lives a long way from Buzby Beach the rest of the year. I hope Jacques doesn't become too attached, only to have his heart broken when Scarlett leaves.

About quarter of nine, the power flickered back on. Jacques cleaned out the coffee maker and brewed a fresh pot.

Nine O'Clock came, but no Kelly, and no Nine O'Clock Club. Kelly texted to say she'd be along shortly since they'd just about finished cleaning up the wreck on the bridge. Jacques was surprised the Nine O'Clock Club didn't show up. They never missed a morning.

"I guess this storm was too much, even for them," he said to Marie.

Marie pointed out the window. "Don't count them out yet."

Pulling into the parking spot next to Kaitlynn's pink Jeep was a dark gray Chevy Tahoe. As Jacques watched, the four doors opened, four umbrellas popped out, and the four ladies of the Nine O'Clock Club stepped daintily over the water running down the gutter, and onto the sidewalk. Before they could reach the door, Jacques was there holding it open for them.

"Thank you, young man," Mrs. Plantain, first through the door, said. Mrs. Kelly and Mrs. Anderson smiled and nodded at him.

"I must say," said Mrs. Lambert, the fourth member of the Nine O'Clock Club – a retired teacher who'd taught Jacques' seventh grade math class – as she came inside. "All this rain, young man."

She looked at Jacques like the rain must be his fault.

"Sorry 'bout that, Mrs. Lambert."

"Well, I guess it's not your fault, is it?" she said, gracing him with a smile and a pat on the shoulder.

Leaning her umbrella against the window sill next to those of her friends, Mrs. Lambert joined the other ladies at their usual table.

Marie came out from behind the counter, trailed by Scarlett, and approached their table.

"Ladies, there was some trouble on the bridge this morning and Kelly's running a bit late.

This is Scarlett. Today's her first day, and she'd be glad to take your order."

Scarlett stepped forward, holding an order pad, and smiled.

"G-good morning, l-ladies."

There was an awkward moment of silence as the Nine O'Clock Club took note of Scarlett's scar and misshapen nose.

Then Mrs. Lambert smiled, and said, "It's nice to meet you Scarlett. First day, eh. Well don't be nervous. We'll go easy on you."

The other ladies in the club echoed Mrs. Lambert's greeting and reassurance. Scarlett, who had started to wilt under their combined gazes, smiled her half-smile and took their orders.

The ladies all placed their regular orders.

Jacques whispered to Scarlett as she handed him the order, "I hope I can make them the way Kelly does."

Scarlett looked back over her shoulder at the club ladies.

"I'm sure you'll d-do fine. They seem like nice ladies."

Jacques knew it was just a coincidence that a loud peal of thunder rumbled just as Scarlett said the Nine O'Clock Club were nice ladies. Scarlett scowled at the grin that curled his lips.

"Wait until you get to know them," he whispered to Scarlett.

Kelly blew through the door just as the rain, which had lightened up considerably, began coming down in sheets again. It was being driven diagonally down the street by the wind. Kelly had to push the door shut against the gale.

"Are you kidding me?" she said, shaking the water off her raincoat.

Spotting the Nine O'Clock Club already sipping on their teas, Kelly walked over to their table.

"Sorry I'm late, ladies. I hope Jacques's taking good care of you."

Mrs. Plantain set her cup down carefully. "Actually, Scarlett there has been taking care of us, and doing a fine job of it, too."

"Indeed she has," Mrs. Lambert added. "And it's kind of cute, her being Jacques' girlfriend and all, the two of them working together."

Kelly's lips twisted in confusion. She turned and saw Scarlett standing by the cake case.

Scarlett's lips twitched as she tried to smile at Kelly, and she gave a hesitant little wave.

Kelly forced a smile on her face and turned back to the ladies. "I'm glad to hear she's been doing her job so well. I'll have to let Marie know you approve."

"Please do," Mrs. Anderson said. "But we're glad to see you, Kelly. I have to admit, we were a bit worried. What with this storm and all."

Kelly looked out the window and licked her lips. "It's sure a bad storm all right. Gale warnings all up and down the coast. I guess that's what happened on the bridge."

"What exactly did happen on the bridge?" Mrs. Lambert asked. "We'd heard it was closed for quite a while due to some kind of accident."

"I couldn't exactly tell from where I was sitting in the line of traffic waiting to cross," Kelly said. "But on the radio they said a camper trailer had been blown across the bridge into the oncoming lanes by a ferocious gust of wind."

"Oh my goodness," Mrs. Kelly said. "Was anyone hurt?"

Kelly tilted her head and shrugged. "Not that I heard. News said the camper was a total loss, though. If the pile of junk on the roll-back I saw going by was the camper, I'd say it was."

Kelly left the ladies conjecturing on the accident and headed to the closet they called an office in the storage room. She smiled and nodded at Scarlett as she walked past, but said nothing.

When Kelly was down the hall, Scarlett walked over to Jacques.

"I d-don't think she l-likes me," Scarlett said, keeping her voice low.

"It's not that. She's just had a rough morning, what with the storm and that deal with the bridge. And she had no idea you were working here."

"Yeah, b-but, the way she looked at me," Scarlett said. "I d-don't think she's t-too happy I waited on those ladies."

"Maybe not," Jacques said.

"B-big help you are," Scarlett said, bumping him with her hip.

"I just meant she might feel a little possessive about the Nine O'Clockers," Jacques said. "Kelly's been taking care of them ever since they started coming in."

"How long is that?" Scarlett asked.

"A while," Jacques replied.

His eyes narrowed, and he stared out the window. "Looks like it's lightening up out there. Maybe the storms blowing on out of here."

"Don't get your hopes up," Kelly said, walking up behind him. "The Weather Channel was showing this thing reaches all the way back to the Gulf, with occasional breaks. It could go on all day."

The storm did go on most of the day, though not with the intensity it showed in the morning. Cameron came in on time at noon, and Marie told Scarlett and Jacques to take off.

"Where do you want to go?" Jacques asked Scarlett while they stood on the sidewalk watching the drizzle.

CHAPTER ELEVEN

Scarlett bit her lip and looked towards The Beach Cone.

"I guess I ought to go see what Kaitlynn's doing. Looks like we missed church. She might want to get home so we can go shopping with Trish and Marissa."

The electronic eye signaled the electric buzzer to imitate a bell sound when they walked into The Cone.

"Welcome to The Beach Cone. What can I…oh. It's just you guys," Kaitlynn said from behind the counter. "You want some ice cream?"

Jacques looked at Scarlett, who shook her head and said, "No, thanks. We just came to see how you were doing."

"Actually, I'm having a great time. AW's been showing me how to do everything. We just turned on the OPEN sign a minute ago. I thought you guys were our first customers."

Mr. Mumples came out from the back. He looked expectantly at Jacques and Scarlett, but his face fell when they turned out not to be customers.

"Hey, Jacques, Scarlett. Are you guys hungry? I've got the fixings ready for turkey and Swiss on rye. That's today's lunch special."

Scarlett perked up at that. "That I'm h-hungry for," she said. "Then maybe after we c-can sample some of K-kait's ice cream handiwork."

"Ginger," Mr. Mumples called toward the back of the shop. "We've got lunch customers."

Ginger came out from the back, wearing a tight white t-shirt emblazoned with an ice cream cone covering most of the front and the words BEACH CONE forming an arc across the top of the cone where the ice cream would be.

"Hi guys," she said to Jacques and Scarlett. "You guys gonna get some lunch?"

"The special your dad was telling us about sounds good," Jacques said. "I'll have that."

"Me, t-too," Scarlett said.

"Coming right up," Ginger said, writing their order down on her pad before walking over to the counter and handing the ticket to her dad.

Jacques watched her walk away, admiring how well the pink shorts that were part of her Beach Cone uniform fit. When he turned back to Scarlett, her head was tilted to one side, her right eyebrow was arched, and her lips were pressed thin.

Jacques swallowed hard, shrugged, and gave her a big-puppy-eyed stare in apology. Scarlett laughed and reached across the table to take his hand. In a bold move, he lifted her hand to his lips and was about to kiss it when a loud fake cough came from the direction of the ice cream counter.

"Excuse me," Kaitlynn said. "Something caught in my throat."

Jacques and Scarlett grinned at each other, but he lowered her hand to the table unkissed; though he didn't relinquish his hold.

Mr. Mumples handed their sandwiches to Ginger almost as soon as she laid the ticket on the counter: two turkey and Swiss on seedless rye, garnished with tomato, lettuce, and a slice of onion, with a side of wavy potato chips.

"Don't forget to ask them what they want to drink," he said quietly to Ginger as she picked up the plates.

Ginger almost dropped the plates when the door buzzer went off as Tony walked in.

"Hey, Ging…whoa…sorry," Tony said, reaching out to steady the plates before they fell. Ginger chuckled, her face reddening.

"It's okay. No problem. Thanks."

Tony rested his hand lightly on her shoulder.

"Okay. I'll go take a seat over there," he said, pointing to the stools along the counter.

Ginger delivered the plates to Jacques and Scarlett without further incident, took their drink orders, and hurried to the counter to take Tony's order. Scarlett nudged Jacques's leg under the table and signaled with a tilt of her head toward Kaitlynn. Kaitlynn was unabashedly checking Tony out.

Jacques laughed into his napkin. "I think he's taken. Him and Ginger. It was love at first sight."

"Isn't he a little old for her?" Scarlett asked.

Jacques' lips twisted into a semi-scowl. "She's sixteen and he's barely nineteen. That's not too big a difference I guess." His scowl turned into a chuckle. "She'll be a junior next year. He's just a sophomore."

Scarlett's eyes went wide. "Tony's gonna be a sophomore?"

Jacques nodded. "At Cape Fear Community College. Gotcha."

Scarlett kicked him under the table.

Tony took his lunch to-go. He'd ordered for both him and his dad. On his way out he stopped at Jacques' table.

"Y'all very busy this morning?" Tony asked Jacques.

Jacques shook his head. "Not really. Slow for a Sunday. Between the storm and the bridge, I guess." Tony glanced over his shoulder in the direction of the bridge.

"Yeah, I guess. We've been dead, but this afternoon maybe the weather will clear and we'll do some business."

"I hope you do," Jacques said.

Then his eyes lit up and he looked at Scarlett. "Have you ever ridden in a surrey?"

Scarlett scrunched her brow, puzzled. "A surrey? I d-don't think so. What is it?"

Tony said, “It’s like a four-wheeled bike with a soft-top. You pedal it like a bike, but drive it like a car. We rent ‘em over at the shop.”

“That sounds l-like fun,” Scarlett said.

“Maybe we can rent one and take a ride if the rain lets up,” Jacques said. “Then I can really show you the island.”

“Why don’t you just rent a couple -” Tony started to ask, but stopped when he caught the subtle shake of Jacques’ head. “Yeah, you’d like the surrey. They’re a blast.”

After Tony left, Scarlett gave Jacques a withering look. “I can ride a bike you know. Just not very fast.”

Jacques was unfazed. “That’s not why I wanted to use a surrey. Surreys have bench seats,” he said as he patted the bench next to him.

“I don’t see why that…oh,” Scarlett said, a shy smile replacing her indignant expression.

“If we’re lucky, we can get one with a fringe on the top,” Jacques said.

Scarlett shook her head, and then took another bite of her sandwich.

Jacques and Scarlett didn’t get to ride in a surrey. The rain never quit for long enough. Scarlett and Kaitlynn left shortly after lunch to pick up Trish and Marissa for their delayed trip to the mall. Ginger had to work until the shop closed, so Jacques decided to head across the street and see what Cienna was up to.

“My mom and I were gonna head over to the theater to see that new movie RIVER DREAM,” Cienna told

Jacques when he asked her what she was up to. "You wanna come?"

Ordinarily, Jacques wouldn't have been interested in seeing a romantic comedy, but there wasn't much else to do around the island on a rainy Sunday afternoon.

"Sure, I'll go. I just need to call my mom and let her know where I'll be."

It was only a couple of blocks to the cinema so they walked even though it was still raining. Cienna's mom had a big blue and white golf umbrella all three of them could fit under. Jacques carried it otherwise he would have had to crouch the entire way.

A long line awaited them outside the cinema.

"I guess we should have expected that," Soon Lee said. "Why don't you kids go ahead and see the movie? I think I'll head over to Shirley's and see what's new."

Soon Lee took the umbrella, seeing as the kids were more-or-less sheltered under the awning that covered most of the sidewalk in front of the cinema. A year before Jacques wouldn't have given a second thought to going to the movies alone with Cienna. Now that he and Scarlett were together, the idea made him feel uncomfortable.

Noticing the way he began to fidget, Cienna asked, "Is something wrong? You need to go to the bathroom or something?"

"No!" Jacques said. "It's nothing. I'm just bored waiting for the line to go down."

Cienna shrugged and turned back toward the ticket booth.

Jacques cell phone vibrated in his pocket. Jacques bit his lip and slowly pulled the phone out, running his finger across the screen to unlock it. He'd received a text. Hoping it wasn't from Scarlett, he dragged the icon down the screen.

With a mixture of relief and disappointment, he saw the message wasn't from Scarlett. His friend Rex, who was away at Camp Riversail for two weeks, had sent him a message.

Is it rainin there 2? Started here last night and won't quit. No sailing, too much wind and lightning. Sucks.

Jacques sent back, **Been rain here since early am. Slow at work. Wreck on bridge 2. Other than rain, hows camp?**

Rex replied, **Good. Got me out of last week of school. Lots more work being in CIT program. Feels like boot camp, lol. Much goin on @ home.**

Jacques laughed at Rex's comparison to the Counselor-in-Training program being like boot camp. He'd told Jacques all about how he'd be getting up early, running, swimming, and who knew what else as part of his training to be a Camp Counselor. It hadn't sounded like much fun to Jacques.

Not much. New ice cream place opened next to Bean. Owner's girl our grade. You'd like her. Pretty cute. Cienna's back 4 2 wks. Met new girl, inlander, we're kind of going out.

Rex's reply wasn't long in coming.

U r goin out with inlander? NAME? STATS? Not the Cienna chik?

Jacques laughed out loud. Cienna turned around and gave him a puzzled look.

"Who's that? Scarlett?"

Cienna's inflection when she said "Scarlett" caught Jacques' ear.

"No, not Scarlett. It's my friend Rex. Do you remember him? He's at camp and it's raining so he's got nothing to do."

Cienna let out a breath she didn't realize she'd been holding.

"Oh. I remember Rex: tall, athletic, loved sailing. Tell him I said 'hey'."

Jacques wasn't going to let her off the hook so easy.

"What if it had been Scarlett? Why would that bother you?"

Cienna pushed her hair behind her ear. "I didn't say it bothered me. I was just wondering, that's all."

She turned her back on him and inched ever closer to the ticket booth. Jacques' phone buzzed in his hand.

U stil there?

Still here, Jacques replied. **Not Cienna chik. Name's Scarlett. From near Asheville. Sister lives in Wilm. Goes 2 UNCW.**

Scarlett goes UNCW?

NO, sister goes 2 UNCW.

O, lol. She w/u now?

No. Went 2 mall w/sister. At movies w/Cienna.

Wait 1. G/F @ mall w/sister. U @ movie w/Cienna. U dawg.

Jacques shook his head.

Not like that. Cienna & me j/f. Her mom w/us but went 2 Shirley's cause line 2 long.

Jacques didn't want Rex thinking Cienna and him were anything but just friends.

Scarlett knos u @ movie with Cienna?

No. Kind of last minute thing. NBD.

Jacques didn't want Rex making a big deal out of things. Rex had a tendency to do that, make big deals out of things.

U say so, man. Gotta run. Duty calls. Later.

Jacques sent, **Later**, figuring Rex had probably already turned off his phone. From what his best friend had told him, phones had to stay in the cabin, turned off, except during break time. He'd been keeping track of Cienna out of the corner of his eye. Now she was staring at him.

"My mom took off with all my money."

She bit her lip and looked to Jacques' left and right before meeting his eyes again.

"Can you cover my ticket? I'll pay you back."

"I got it," Jacques said. "Don't worry about it."

"I'll pay you back," Cienna said. "It's just that my mom has my money in her purse."

"It's no big deal," Jacques said. "I don't mind getting your ticket."

Cienna put her hand on her hip. "You might not mind. You sure Scarlett wouldn't mind?"

"I'm sure if Scarlett was here she'd insist I help you out," Jacques said, with more confidence than he felt.

He hadn't known Scarlett long, barely two days. She might not even like him being there with Cienna at all.

"Besides, you said you'd pay me back, so it's just a loan, right?"

"Right," Cienna said. "It's not like we're on a date or something."

Because you had to go and find a girlfriend the day I came back. Talk about bad timing.

Cienna hadn't told Jacques, but her pending breakup with Josh wasn't exactly pending as much as a done deal, and had been for six months. She'd told Josh to take a hike when he tried to insist she go all the way and hadn't wanted to take "NO" for an answer. She'd explained that she was breaking up with him while he lay in the fetal position moaning and holding his privates. She'd never told her dad, figuring she'd handled it herself, and Josh never mentioned it, or called her again.

It wasn't until the family began packing to come to Buzby Beach that Cienna's started thinking about Jacques. The closer they got to the beach, the more she thought about him. Then when she got to Buzby Beach, the very day, Jacques found a girlfriend.

Jacques watched Cienna's face as the thoughts roiling around in her head showed in her eyes. He wasn't sure what the look meant, but it made him uneasy.

"No, it's not like we're on a date. Not that being on a date with you wouldn't be cool. If I wasn't with Scarlett. I mean, I'm with you...here, but I'm...she's my...."

"Oh just shut up Jacques, and pay for our tickets," Cienna said, turning away from him to hide the emotion on her face.

Jacques clamped his mouth shut, pointed to the placard advertising the teen romance, RIVER DREAM, and held up two fingers. The clerk, a girl he recognized from South Hanover High, but didn't really know, smirked at him and told him he owed twelve bucks. Jacques handed her a twenty and she counted out his change before handing him the two tickets.

"Enjoy the movie," the clerk said automatically, before instantly forgetting him and turning her attention to the next person in line.

Jacques held the door for Cienna and handed their tickets to the red-jacketed usher, who tore them and handed Jacques back the halves.

"You're in Cinema Two; enjoy the movie."

"Do you want some popcorn or something?"

"Are you sure Scarlett would insist you buy your not-a-date popcorn?" Cienna said, and immediately regretted it when she saw the hurt in Jacques' eyes.

He turned and walked toward Cinema Two. "Just forget it then."

Cienna ran after him and grabbed his arm. "I'm sorry. I shouldn't have said that. I was being a jerk. I'd really like some popcorn, and a soda?"

Jacques felt torn inside, like he was trying to turn in both directions at once.

I've got a girlfriend now. I'm not supposed to feel like this about Cienna. What's the matter with me?

To Cienna he said, "Okay, let's get some popcorn. You want to share a large?"

Cienna smiled, and put her arm through his. "Yeah, that would be okay. And a diet Coke."

Jacques glanced down at her arm through his. It felt wrong and right at the same time.

"We should probably each have our own Coke."

"Ew, yes," Cienna said.

They took seats half-way back, center of the row. The old theater didn't boast stadium seating. The advertisements that preceded the previews were still looping when they sat down.

"So what's this movie about anyway?" Jacques leaned toward Cienna and whispered.

Cienna turned so her mouth was just inches from his ear.

"It's about these two kids who grow up together at Wrightsville Beach, and how it takes them forever to figure out they love each other. I heard the guy who wrote the book grew up in Wilmington."

"Really," Jacques said.

He was trying to ignore the electric sensation her breath upon his ear was having on his body.

"Too bad it wasn't Mr. Warren. If one of his books got made into a movie he'd have enough money to ask my mom out to someplace nice."

Cienna shoved Jacques' shoulder. "Get out. Mr. Warren wants to hook-up with…er…go out with your mom?"

"What's wrong with that?" Jacques said. "There's nothing wrong with my mom."

"Hey," Cienna said. "I love your mom. It's Mr. Warren. The two of them together. I don't see it."

Before Jacques could respond, the lights dimmed and the exits announcement came on. By the time the movie was over, and the stars had professed their love for one another while standing on a windswept pier on a brisk December morning, Cienna's arm was firmly curled around Jacques', their fingers entwined, and her head on his shoulder.

The fact that such a situation was wholly inappropriate for a boy to find himself in when the girl in question wasn't his girlfriend didn't hit Jacques until the credits finished running and the lights came up. Almost on cue, his phone vibrated in his pocket.

Cienna sat up as if hit with an electric shock.

"Oh…um…oh, I guess we oughta go."

Jacques glanced at his screen. He'd received another text. Dragging his finger across the screen and pulling down the icon, he saw that this one was from Scarlett. He put the phone back in his pocket without reading it.

"Yeah, I guess we'd better."

After a quick pit stop, they met in front of the theater. The rain had stopped, but the sun was still lost behind a thinning cover of clouds, making the sky brighter than it had been, but leaving open the question of whether the rain was done with them.

"Who was the text from?" Cienna asked, carefully keeping an arm's length from Jacques.

"I haven't checked yet," he lied.

"Don't you think you should? Could be your mom."

Jacques knew it wasn't his mom. He pulled out his phone and read the text.

"It's from Scarlett," he said. "They're done at the mall. She's wondering what I'm doing."

Cienna nodded. "What are you going to tell her?"

Jacques was busy typing. After he hit send, he told Cienna, "I told her I just caught a movie with a friend."

"Did you tell her I was the friend?" Cienna asked, looking at the sidewalk in front of him rather than at Jacques.

"Yes," Jacques said. "I did."

"What did she say about that?" Jacques looked at his phone.

"I don't know yet."

They stood there on the walk, people passing to either side of them, waiting for his phone to buzz again.

That's nice. What movie?

"She wants to know what movie," Jacques said.

Cienna watched him type, saying nothing.

River Dream, by that guy from around here.

Was it any good?

"She wants to know if it was any good."

"I liked it," Cienna said, moving closer so she could see his screen. "Did you like it?"

Jacques shrugged. "It was okay."

That's what he sent to Scarlett.

Good date movie?

"She wants to know -"

"I can see the screen, Jacques."

"Oh."

"Well, what are you going to tell her?" Cienna asked.

Jacques wrinkled his nose. "I don't know. I've never actually taken a date to a movie. How do I know if it was a good date movie?"

"If, by the end of the movie, your date has her arm wrapped around yours, is holding your hand, and has her head on your shoulder, then it was probably a pretty good date movie," Cienna said, her voice strained.

Jacques flinched as if she'd hit him. Before he could reply, she stomped off.

Jacques phone buzzed again.

U still at movie?

On way home.

Stop in at Cone.

Jacques stomach knotted.

U there?

K wanted 2 show T & M. Mr. M offered K regular job.

Jacques looked up the street toward home.

B there in 5. xo

Jacques hoped the 'xo' would help get him out of the doghouse he figured he was in for being at the movies with Cienna when Scarlett showed up at The Bean.

Scarlett, Kaitlynn, Trish, and Marissa were sitting in the very booth he and Scarlett shared lunch in. Cienna was at the counter telling Ginger about the movie.

"You've gotta get Tony to take you," Jacques overheard Cienna say as the buzzer announced his entrance to The Cone.

All the girls' heads turned and watched him walk in. Deliberately ignoring Cienna and Ginger, Jacques went straight to the table where Scarlett was sitting.

"Hi," he said, with a sort of half-wave of his hand at his waist. "Didn't think I'd see you until tomorrow."

Trish coughed, "Obviously," into her napkin.

Scarlett gave her a dirty look, and got up from the table.

"Let's sit over there," she said, pointing to an empty table near the back. "It's not as c-crowded."

After they sat down, Scarlett reached across the table and took Jacques' hand. "You think I'm mad at you, d-don't you?"

Jacques' eyes were on their hands. "Aren't you?"

Scarlett leaned across the table. "Should I b-be?"

Forcing himself not to let his eyes shift left toward Cienna and Ginger, Jacques said, "I don't think so. You're not mad I went to the movie with Cienna?"

"You went as friends, right? That's all, right?"

Jacques' tongue darted across his lips. Fighting the urge to glance at Cienna literally hurt his neck. "That's all it was. We're, Cienna and me, we're just friends."

From the counter they could hear Cienna say, "I wish I'd been there with a boy I really like, you know, like that. It was such a romantic movie."

Scarlett glanced at Cienna, smiled, and looked back at Jacques.

"D-do you wish you'd b-been there with a g-girl you really like, you know, like that?"

Jacques turned his hand over and squeezed hers gently. "I wish I'd been there with you."

He leaned across the table toward her. She didn't pull back. Gently, his lips met hers. Scarlett's lips parted, just slightly, and Jacques' tongue played tentatively along her lips before retreating. No sisterly cough interrupted them. The door buzzer buzzing as Cienna exited did.

Jacques and Scarlett fell back into their chairs, her eyes closed and a satisfied smile on her face; him watching Cienna look both ways before running across the street to The News Stand. Out of the corner of his eye, he caught Ginger shaking her head at him.

CHAPTER TWELVE

Across the street at The News Stand, Cienna's grandmother looked up from the magazine she was reading as Cienna burst in the door.

"Well, there you are. Your mom came back ages ago. She told me she ditched you kids at the theater. So, how was the mo - goodness, honey. What's wrong?"

Cienna sniffed and wiped her eyes with the back of her hand. "Boys are so stupid."

"Boys," Grandma Philbert said. "Are you talking about Jacques? Dear, what happened?"

Cienna took a deep breath, and stifled her sniffles. "I don't know. We went to the movie. He paid my way, and even bought me popcorn. The movie was very romantic, and we wound up holding hands. Then he gets a text from his girlfriend and goes all weird on me."

Grandma Philbert's lips twisted into a frown. "I'm afraid I'm a bit confused, dear. Jacques's got a girlfriend, but paid your way into a movie and the two of you were holding hands. Why did he do that if he has a girlfriend? I didn't know Jacques even had a girlfriend."

Cienna shook her head. "He just met her the other day, Friday, the day I got here. He wasn't supposed to do that."

Cienna's mom came out from the back room in time to hear the last thing Cienna said. "Who wasn't supposed to do what?" she asked.

"Jacques," Cienna said. "He wasn't supposed to go and get himself a girlfriend until after I got here and decided whether I liked him that way."

Grandmother and mother exchanged a knowing look.

Soon Lee said, "I didn't think you felt that way about Jacques. You always said he was just a good friend. When did this all happen?"

Cienna sniffed and shrugged. "When I got here, I guess. When I first saw him again. Or maybe I realized it when he introduced me to Ginger and I thought he liked her, and I didn't want him to."

"How serious are things with him and this new girlfriend?" Grandma Philbert asked.

"I don't know," Cienna said. "Pretty serious I guess. They were kissing in The Cone."

Grandma Philbert's eyes got wide. "Jacques was kissing a girl in the ice cream parlor? I wonder what Marie would have to say about that."

Cienna shook her head and grabbed her grandmother's arm. "Please, don't say anything. I don't want him to get in any trouble."

Back in The Beach Cone, Kaitlynn was telling Scarlett, "We need to get going. You're supposed to Skype Mom and Dad tonight."

Scarlett rose reluctantly from her seat, as did Jacques from his.

"I c-can't wait t-to t-tell them all about you, Jacques. Hey, d-do you have Skype?"

"No," Jacques said, shaking his head. "My laptop's kind of old. It doesn't have a webcam."

"B-bummer," Scarlett said. "If you d-did, we c-could Skype after I t-talk to my p-parents."

"That'd be cool," Jacques said. "But like I said, my laptop don't have a camera."

Jacques walked Scarlett out to Kaitlynn's Jeep, and stole another quick kiss before Kaitlynn backed out and they drove off. He thought about going back into The Cone, but decided to head home and see what his mom had planned for dinner.

"I thought we'd drive into town and have dinner at Outback," Marie said when Jacques asked. "How's that sound?"

"It sounds great to me," Jacques said, a big smile curling his lips. "You know I love their ribs."

"And after dinner I thought we'd pick up a few things at Wal-Mart."

Jacques laughed. "I knew there'd be a catch."

They walked the short distance to Island Self-Storage where Marie kept her truck - a mint condition, blue and white 1967 Ford F-150 pickup that once belonged to Jacques' grandfather. The truck technically belonged to Jacques, like the building where The Parisian Bean was located, but as his trustee and Mother, Marie could use it whenever she needed. In the stall next to the truck was Marie's car, a classic 1968 Pontiac Firebird Convertible left behind by Jacques' father when he walked out on them.

After dinner and shopping, Jacques and Marie unloaded the groceries and supplies from the truck before parking it back in its stall at Island Self-Storage. Walking back from the storage place, Marie brought up the subject of Jacques and Scarlett.

"JQ, just how serious are things getting with you and Scarlett?"

Jacques looked down at his feet as they walked up Seventh Street. "Not too serious, I guess. I mean, I really like her a lot, but it's not like I'm gonna ask her to marry me or nothing."

"Well, that's good. That you're not planning on asking her to marry you, I mean. You've only known her a few days."

Jacques shrugged, but didn't say anything.

Marie changed the subject. "How was that movie you and Cienna went to? Any good?"

"Yeah," Jacques said. "It was all right. Cienna liked it more than I did."

"How did Scarlett like you going to a romantic movie with Cienna?" Marie asked.

"She was cool with it," Jacques said. "She knows Cienna and I are just friends."

"That's good, I guess," Marie said, "that Scarlett's cool with you being friends with cute girls like Cienna."

"Yeah, I guess," Jacques said. He looked up at his mom. "Cienna is kind of cute, ain't she?"

"Isn't she," Marie said.

Jacques rolled his eyes, but Marie pretended not to notice.

"Yes, Jacques. She's quite pretty. I'm surprised you haven't noticed."

"I've noticed," Jacques said, as the waited for the light to change at the corner of Seventh and Sound Streets.

The light changed, they crossed over to their side of Sound Street and turned south toward The Bean. Mr. Mumples was locking up The Beach Cone as they walked by.

"Hi, AW," Marie said. "Good crowd tonight?"

"Not bad," Mr. Mumples said, dropping his keys in his pocket. "Things picked up once the rain quit. We had a pretty good night. Last customers just left a little while ago."

"Glad to hear it's going well. It's good having y'all next door."

Mr. Mumples smiled before turning towards the alley next to The Cone where he parked his car. "Thanks, Marie."

Marie and Jacques continued down the street, past the closed coffee shop, FITU2A-T, and the shuttered

Buzby Beach Bikes, finally reaching the stairs to the apartments.

"Jacques," Marie asked as she unlocked the door to the stairway, "do you ever wish we lived in a regular house, like the Mumples?"

"Not really," Jacques replied. "I kind of like living over The Bean. Especially now that the Sand Bar is gone."

He laughed and Marie joined him.

A short time later, in his room, Jacques booted up his laptop. Once it finished booting up, he logged into his Facebook account. When he saw he had a message, Jacques felt a chill, thinking it might be another from his father. It wasn't. It was from Kaitlynn. Jacques clicked to open it.

Jacques,

I'm so sorry to have to tell you this. Scarlett can't see you anymore. When she told our parents about you, my dad went ballistic. He wouldn't listen to anything she tried to tell him about you. I'm sorry. He left tonight to pick her up and take her back to Canton tomorrow.

He got all on my case about not looking out for her and letting her get involved with, I'm quoting him, "a local beach bum, looking for an easy score."

Jacques, I know you're not like that. Scarlett does too. She made me promise to get this message to you. Our father made me take her

phone. He'll check it when he gets here to make sure she didn't contact you.

Scarlett's been crying since they signed off. She really likes you, Jacques. And I know you like her. All I can say is, I'm sorry.

Kaitlynn

Jacques stared at the message, a cold weight settling in his stomach, bile rising in his throat, tears brimming in his eyes. He hurt. A whimper escaped his throat. He rocked back and forth in his chair. That's how he was when Marie knocked on his door to say good-night.

"Jacques, honey. What's wrong?"

Thinking he'd gotten another message from his father, Marie read the message, still open on his screen. When she finished, Marie put her arms around him.

"Oh, Jacques, I'm so sorry. Who does that son-of-a-bitch think he is, saying that about you? I'm so sorry."

Safe in his mother's arms, Jacques let the tears he'd been trying to hold back flow. He cried out the pain and hurt that Kaitlynn's message had delivered along with the news that he'd never be able to see Scarlett again.

Jacques couldn't understand how Scarlett's father could hate him when he didn't even know him. Marie stayed with him until he finally fell asleep.

The next morning, sunshine streaming past his blinds woke Jacques up.

"Sunshine. Oh crap. I overslept," Jacques said to his window. He looked at his alarm clock and saw that it had been turned off.

"Who turned that off?" he asked himself. Then the memory of the message from Kaitlynn surfaced in his mind.

Jacques climbed from bed, realized he was still in the clothes he'd worn to dinner with his mom the night before, and opened his laptop.

"Mom must have shut you down," he said to the computer.

Jacques started to push the button to boot it back up, but stopped himself.

"What's the point? It's not like the message disappeared overnight. It's over. It was short, it was sweet, and it's over."

His heart wasn't as easily convinced as his head. It hung heavy in his chest, like a lead balloon.

Jacques dragged himself through his morning routine. Eventually, he went down to The Bean. The sunshine that greeted him when he walked outside momentarily blinded him.

"Morning, JQ," Mr. Bishop called out. "What's new with you?"

"Morning, Mr. Bishop," Jacques said so softly Mr. Bishop barely heard him.

"Hey, Jacques," Tony said. "You gonna need that surrey today? I'll try and hold one for you if you want."

Jacques stared at Tony for a moment, wondering why Tony would hold one of the four-wheel bikes for him. His stomach twisted when he remembered.

"No thanks, Tony. I won't be needing it."

"You all right, Jacques?" Tony asked. "You don't look so good."

"Rough night," Jacques said. "I kinda don't wanna talk about it."

"Okay, man. I'll, uh, talk to you later."

Jacques nodded and walked on toward The Bean.

Kelly greeted him when he walked in. "Morning, sleepy head. About time you showed up for work."

She was delivering a second round of drinks to the Nine O'Clock Club.

Jacques stood in the doorway, puzzled. "Hey, Kelly. What are you doing here? It's Monday, isn't it?"

Kelly delivered the ladies' teas before walking over to Jacques and answering his question. "Your mom called me this morning and asked if I could work today. She thought you might need a day off. Told me you had a rough night."

"Yeah. I guess I did."

"So, why don't you go back upstairs and take it easy? Or maybe go chillax on the beach or something. I got things covered here."

Jacques ran his hand over his head. "I guess you're right. The mood I'm in wouldn't be too good for customer service."

Kelly took him by the shoulders, turned him toward the door, and gave him a push. "Go on, before you start scaring away customers."

Jacques stood on the sidewalk outside The Bean, looking up and down the road, trying to decide what to do. He looked to his left. The Cone wasn't open yet.

Mr. Lemon was just arriving to unlock FITU2A-T. He looked at Jacques and nodded before stepping inside.

Jacques looked across the street at The News Stand. He shook his head. He looked right and headed back to Buzby Beach Bikes.

"Hey, Jacques. Didn't expect to see you back so soon. What do you need?"

"Can I get my bike?" Jacques asked. "I feel like going for a ride."

Tony frowned at him. "Not working today?"

"Nah," Jacques said. "My mom gave me the day off on account of what happened between me and Scarlett."

In response to Tony's puzzled expression, Jacques said, "When her dad found out about me, he drove all night to get here and take her back to the mountains."

"Dude, that sucks." Tony put a hand on Jacques shoulder. "You gonna be all right?"

"Yeah. I'll be okay."

Jacques jumped on his beach cruiser and pedaled south down Sound Street toward The Coastal Towers. He passed Mr. Bagley in the Buzby Beach Bakery truck headed north. Jacques waved and Mr. Bagley tooted his horn.

Swinging past the resort's entrance, Jacques rolled around the corner where Sound Street ended and Ocean Street began. A quarter-mile later, thirsty from his exertions, he pulled into the South End Gas and Grocery. Steering his bike between the Lexus SUV parked in front of the door and the Lincoln Navigator next to it, Jacques leaned his bike against the Propane

Gas Bottle Exchange cage and went inside in search of a bottle of spring water.

Cold bottle of spring water in hand, Jacques stood in front of the store, scowling at the rich inlanders' houses across the street blocking his view of the ocean. He finished off the water and stuffed the bottle through the round opening in the top of the blue trash can labeled "PLASTICS." Casting one last resentful glance at the three-story testaments to man's daring in the face of certain storms to come, Jacques headed north on Ocean Street, past the Mini-Golf and Go-Kart Track, the Arcade, and Iggie's, before stopping at the pier.

There was a bike rack next to the walkway up to the pier and Jacques secured his beach cruiser to it. He was surprised to see Scout behind the counter selling bait and pier passes, until he remembered his mom telling him about Scout's new job.

"Hey, Scout," Jacques said, unable to conjure a smile.

Scout nodded and replied, "JQ."

Scout didn't ask him what he was doing there, or why he seemed so down, and Jacques was glad he didn't. Instead, all Scout asked was, "Goin' fishin'?"

"Not today. Thought I'd just take a walk on the pier."

Jacques noticed a Parisian Bean coffee cup on the counter near Scout. "Stopped by The Bean this morning, huh?"

Scout glanced at the cup, and then nodded at Jacques.

Jacques was half-way down the pier when Marie's ring tone sounded on his phone. He pulled it out and slid his finger across the screen to answer.

"Hi, Mom."

"Hi, JQ. I just thought I'd check in to see if you're okay."

"I'm fine, Mom. I'm at the pier."

"Oh, okay. How'd you get to the pier?"

"I rode my bike." *How'd she think I got here, on the bus?*

"So, you gonna do some fishing?"

"No, ma'am. I just felt like taking a walk on the pier. Thought it might do me some good."

"All right," Marie said. "If you're sure you're okay. Let me know when you leave to come back."

"I will, Mom. Love you."

"I love you too, honey."

CHAPTER THIRTEEN

Jacques hit END, stuffed the phone in his pocket and continued towards the end of the pier. There was a modest crowd of fisherman trying their luck, but Jacques took no notice of the fish being caught. An empty bench two-thirds of the way down the pier beckoned. Jacques sat down on the north facing slab of concrete, leaned back, and put his feet up on the lowest rail.

The pier had been rebuilt after Hurricane Floyd destroyed it in 1999. It was one of three piers destroyed - only two were rebuilt - along the New Hanover County shoreline by that storm. Both rebuilt piers were constructed of concrete, better to withstand future storms.

Jacques barely remembered the old, wooden, Buzby Beach Pier that was knocked down by a hurricane when he was about three, the same year his father left. His mom had pictures of him there as a toddler, fishing with his father and grandfather, but it hardly seemed the same place to him as the gray-white concrete pier he'd grown up with.

The winds were light. The waves rolled gently into the shore in the calm following the previous day's storm. After a time watching the pelicans diving on schools of bait fish, Jacques pulled out his phone and with practiced swipes of his fingers on the screen, called up his Facebook page. He accessed the message from Kaitlynn and read it one more time. It hadn't changed.

Jacques gnawed at his lower lip while his finger hovered over the DELETE icon. Heaving a sigh that shook his shoulders, he lowered his finger, and the message disappeared.

"Well, I guess that's that," he said to the waves.

Deleting the message did little to delete the hurt and confusion he felt over how Scarlett had been so abruptly removed from his life. Jacques couldn't understand why her father would react like he did just because Scarlett was hanging out with him.

Had Scarlett told her father about the kissing? Had Kaitlynn?

Jacques realized he'd probably never know.

With another shoulder shaking sigh, Jacques heaved himself from the bench and started back to the pier house.

He unlocked his bike from the rack and was almost to Center Street when he spotted Cienna coming down the other side of the street on a bright green Buzby Beach

Bike. She turned around in front of Los Amigos Mexican Restaurante when she saw Jacques and caught up to him at the light.

"Hey," Cienna said when she pulled her bike up next to his.

"Hi," Jacques replied, not looking at her.

"I went to The Bean to see if you wanted to hang out after work, but your mom said you had the day off."

Jacques turned her way just enough to see her out of the corner of his eye. "Yeah. She gave me the day off."

"Oh. I asked her if you were hanging out with Scarlett and...she...she kind of told me what happened."

Cienna leaned away from Jacques as if expecting him to erupt or something. He just sighed and shrugged.

"Kinda sucks," she said

"Yeah, kinda does," Jacques said, pushing his glasses up his nose.

The light changed to green. He pushed off and pedaled through the intersection. Cienna caught up a moment later. They rode along in silence until they reached Sound Street.

"So, you going home?" Cienna asked.

Jacques shrugged. "Thought I might ride up to the Park."

Cienna dared ask, "Mind if I ride along? I haven't been to the Park since I came back."

Jacques was about to tell her he'd rather go alone, but the concern showing in her eyes stayed his tongue. He swung his head in the direction of the Park. "Keep up."

"Ha. Eat my dust, Island Boy."

Her use of the name she'd tagged him with the summer before, borrowed from the Kenny Chesney song, made Jacques smile despite his blue mood.

"That'll be the day, Army Brat," he called in answer to her challenge.

They'd worked up a thirst by the time they reached the Bridge Crossing Stop & Shop.

Cienna pulled into the parking lot with Jacques hot on her heels.

"Drinks are on me," Cienna said. "It's my turn to buy. Whatcha want?"

Jacques held the door for her. As she walked in he said, "Just a bottle of spring water, a big bottle."

"I can do that. Think I'll get one, too."

Cienna paid for their waters. They went outside and sat on the benches alongside the store, where they could see the drawbridge that connected Buzby Beach to the rest of the world.

Jacques drank deeply of his water, and then burped. "Geez. Excuse me all to pieces. Sorry 'bout that."

Cienna took a long pull from her bottle and tried to mimic his belch, without much success.

When he laughed at her, she said, "I guess I'm just not as full of it as you are."

Jacques stopped laughing long enough to say, "You're just out of practice. You got some good one's last summer."

Cienna punched him on the shoulder. "I did not," she said, even though she knew she had. The young lady she'd become since last summer recoiled from acknowledging an aptitude for loud belching.

Jacques wisely chose to let it go.

"I'm getting hungry, Cienna said. "I could use some lunch. What about you?"

"Shrimp, okay?" Jacques asked, referring to Island Shrimp & Seafood next door to the Bridge Crossing.

"They got all you can eat at lunch, right?" Cienna replied. "What are we waiting for?"

Island Shrimp & Seafood, across North Creek from the Buzby Island Marina, boasted its own fleet of shrimp trawlers - three, and fishing boats - four. Mr. Le also had a small fleet of refrigerated trucks that delivered his fresh seafood to stores and restaurants around New Hanover County, but it was the take-out or eat-in restaurant that fronted the fish house that the pair headed for.

"I always love coming in here," Cienna said, taking in the worn wooden floorboards, the bare studs on the walls, the open rafters of the ceiling from which slowly rotating fans hung. "It makes me think of the beach the way it must have been when my dad grew up here."

"It does have kind of an old-timey feel to it," Jacques said.

He knew that Mr. Le had gone to a lot of trouble to make it look that way. The shrimp shack - islanders' unofficial name for the restaurant - had only been added to the seafood company site a half-dozen years before.

Carl Le, Mr. Le's oldest son, whose own daughter was a year ahead of Jacques at South Hanover High, came out from the back in response to the ubiquitous door buzzer.

"What you say, Jacques? How's your momma these days? Still brewing the best coffee on the island?"

Jacques smiled with pride. "She's doing good, Mr. Le."

Carl frowned and shook his finger at Jacques.

"How many times do I hafta tell you Jacques, call me Carl? Mr. Le is the old man out on the dock counting the shrimp."

From the back of the store came a shout of "I heard that." Carl winked at Jacques and put his finger to his lips.

"You look familiar young lady," Carl said to Cienna. "But you're not local, I don't think." When Cienna started to tell him who she was, Carl interrupted, "No, don't tell me. I'll remember."

He squinted hard and leaned his head towards her, his lips pursed. With a start, he stood up straight, clapped his hands and said, "I've got it. Your Reggie Philbert's little girl, Serena."

"Cienna," she said. "Yes, Reggie is my dad."

"That's right, Cienna," Carl said, cringing. "You stay with Bev and Herb during the summer."

"For a couple of weeks," Cienna said. "I'm back for two weeks now, and then we're moving here at the end of summer so we'll be all settled in when my dad retires after he goes to Korea."

"Old Reggie's coming home to stay, eh?" Carl stroked his chin. "I'm not surprised. You know your dad and I graduated South Hanover High together?"

Cienna shook her head. "No, I didn't know that."

"I only went there that one year. Right after my dad went to work here for Old Man Hanson, the guy who used to own this place."

Jacques scratched his head in thought. "Wasn't it you who convinced your dad to open up the shrimp shack?"

"Yeah, that was me. When I moved home after selling my software company to Oracle." Carl laughed.

"He told me if I wanted to spend my money on it, go right ahead. Now that it's making money, he claims it was his idea."

A shout of "I heard that," came again from the back. Carl shook his head and rolled his eyes.

"You two didn't come here to gab about our history. What can I get you?" Carl asked.

Jacques looked at Cienna and raised an eyebrow. She nodded.

"Two shrimp boats, please," Jacques told Carl.

"Coming right up."

He reached under the counter and handed Jacques two drink cups. "You know where the drink machine is."

Jacques and Cienna each had two helpings of the fried shrimp. Bellies full, they said good-bye to Carl and retrieved their bikes.

"Where's your bike?" Jacques asked, gesturing at the bright green Buzby Beach Bikes cruiser Cienna was riding.

"I wasn't about to ride that little bike I had last year," Cienna said, scrunching her nose. "Grandpa told me I should just rent one while I'm here, since I'll be bringing my new bike from home at the end of summer anyway."

Jacques nodded. "That makes sense."

They stood next to the shrimp shack, watching the traffic on Sound Street.

Finally Cienna said, "So, where to now? Towards home, or out to the beach?"

"How about the Park? That's where we were headed anyway."

Cienna put a foot up on the pedal. "Sounds good to me. Let's go."

They rode around the Park, once on the road and once on the trail, before locking their bikes up at the Park Beach parking area and walking out on the sand.

Their shoes in their hands, Jacques and Cienna walked along the water's edge, letting the surf wash over their feet. They strolled in silence; Jacques, his head hung down as thoughts of how short and bittersweet his budding romance with Scarlett wound up being; Cienna, with her eye on Jacques, wondering what she could do to help him feel better.

"Jacques," she said, softly. "Jacques, I'm real sorry about Scarlett having to leave like that. It's not fair to you. You're a great guy, and if her dad would of just bothered to meet you, he'd have known it."

Jacques heaved a sigh and stopped. The surf washed over his feet and almost up to his knees. He turned to look at Cienna.

"Thanks. I don't know why it bothers me so much, really. We only knew each other a few days, but I liked her a lot. And she liked me, too. No other girl ever liked me like that."

Cienna stood rooted to her piece of sand. Her tongue twitched behind her teeth with the urge to tell

Jacques that at least one other girl liked him like that, but she knew it wasn't the right time. She compromised.

"I know it doesn't help much right now, but there'll be other girls. You're a likeable guy, Jacques."

There. Cienna felt she'd said it just right. *When Jacques's ready, he'll figure out what I'm telling him.*

"You really think so?" Jacques asked, a trace of a smile curling his lip.

Cienna punched him playfully on the shoulder. "She's out there, somewhere. Just wait and see."

As they retrieved their bikes from the rack, Jacques remembered he was supposed to call his mom when he was on his way home from the pier.

Technically, I wasn't on my way home when I left the pier.

He pulled his phone out, navigated to his contact favorites, and tapped the screen to call Marie's cell phone.

"Hi, Jacques. Still at the pier?" Marie asked.

"No. I'm at the Park with Cienna. She came and met me by the pier." Jacques rationalized that it was sort of what happened.

"Oh. Did you guys have lunch?"

"We ate at the shrimp shack. Carl said to say hi."

"So, will you be home for supper?" Marie asked.

"We're on our way back now. Shouldn't take us long."

"Is Cienna coming to dinner?"

"No," Jacques said. "Not unless you asked her."

"I was thinking you might have invited her."

"Do you want me to?" Jacques asked. "She's right here."

"It's up to you, JQ. We're just having a salad and some chicken tenders." Something about her tone set off a warning bell in Jacques head.

"Never mind. I'll be home shortly."

"All right. I'll see you shortly."

Jacques wasn't sure why he was angry about how his mother spoke to him on the phone; he just was. He punched END without saying good-bye or telling her he loved her. As soon as the connection was broken, guilt settled into his stomach like a stone. He jammed the phone into his pocket.

CHAPTER FOURTEEN

"We'd better get going," Jacques said in response to Cienna's raised eyebrow. "I think my mom's mad about something."

Cienna replied by pushing off with her foot and heading toward the Park entrance.

Jacques said good-bye to Cienna at Buzby Beach Bikes and headed up the stairs to the apartment. When he walked in, Marie was standing by the stove picking chicken tenders off a baking pan and putting them on the salads she'd prepared for the two of them.

"Hi Mom," Jacques said as he pulled the door closed. "I'm home."

"I can see that, Jacques," Marie said. "I'm more concerned with where you've been all day."

Jacques had been walking toward her, expecting a hug, but her tone stopped him short. "I rode my bike to the pier, and then after, I rode up to the Park and took a walk on the beach."

"So," Marie said, wiping her hands on her apron. "I give you the morning off and you disappear for the whole day."

"The morning off? You told me to take the day off."

"You know I need you on Mondays, Jacques. Kelly and Cameron take the day off. Without you I'm all alone there."

"Mom, Kelly was there when I showed up for work. She's the one who said you told me to take the day off."

Marie put her hands on her hips. "And you thought I meant the whole day? Really, Jacques?"

"If you meant the morning, why didn't you tell Kelly to tell me just the morning?" Jacques felt the heat rising in him, and strained to keep his voice even.

"Don't take that tone with me, young man. I'm your mother and your boss."

"Yeah, well, maybe I don't want my mother to be my boss any more. Maybe I quit."

Marie recoiled as though Jacques had slapped her. Her eyes narrowed and she said sharply, "You quit. You can't quit. You need to pay your way around here, buddy. No free rides."

"Pay my way," Jacques said. "What are you talking about, Mom? Why are you being like this?"

"Me? Why am I being like this?" Marie pushed her hands through her hair.

"You take off all day. I have no idea where you are. And I'm the one being like this."

Jacques stared at his mother. He'd never seen her act that way. He took a deep breath and let it out slowly. "Do you want to tell me what's really wrong? It's not like today's the first day I've spent riding around the island without checking in with you. What's this really all about?"

Marie pointed a finger in Jacques face. "It's about you not showing me the simple courtesy of showing up for work today. It's about you running all over town and not letting me know where you were."

Jacques recoiled at the anger flashing in her eyes. She was starting to scare him. And make him mad. Marie continued her rant.

"It's about you thinking you can do what you please and go where you please and get away with anything and I'll be there to pay the bills."

Jacques decided he'd had enough. "With whose money, Mom?"

Marie blinked. "What do you mean?"

Jacques drove in relentlessly. "Pay the bills with whose money, Mom? Grandpa left me the building. So technically, I own the apartment. All the stores pay rent, except The Bean. And the tenants, too. So where's all the money paying all those bills. You keep telling me The Bean barely turns a profit every month, right. So it must be my money, from the rent on my building, that pays all those bills you're talking about. Ain't that right?"

Marie stood speechless. She looked at Jacques like she'd just realized it was her son in front of her.

"Oh, Jacques, I'm so sorry."

Tears started rolling down her cheeks.

Jacques head spun in confusion. "What are…sorry…sorry about what?"

She pulled him into her arms and held him close. "I was so worried about you. First that message from your father, and then the news about Scarlett. I've been worried sick all day about you."

"I'm okay, Mom. Really. And I'm sorry, too. Sorry I said those things. I didn't mean it.Really, I didn't."

Jacques began to cry, too.

By the time they'd collected themselves and sat down to eat, the chicken tenders were cold. Jacques and Marie didn't care. They didn't even notice.

After supper, Marie popped popcorn and they sat together on the couch and watched Phineas and Ferb on Disney On-Demand. When Marie finally announced she was going to bed, Jacques went to his room and booted up his laptop.

Jacques was hoping to see a message from Scarlett, explaining what had happened with her dad, but there was nothing from her. Cienna had left him a message though. He glanced at the right side of the page, saw a green dot next to her name, and typed a message into the chat box.

U there?

Jacques waited for her to reply. It took so long, he started thinking maybe she'd gone to bed and forgotten to log off. Finally, he saw the words "Cienna typing" on the chat box.

Here. Howd it go w/ur mom

Jacques wondered how much to tell her. Not all of it that was for sure.

She was kind of worried. U kno moms. Worryin makes em mad.

Tell me bout it. Mine wanted to ground me for not showing up til supper

Jacques felt a twinge of guilt for Cienna getting in trouble because she'd been with him.

Hope shes not 2 mad. Tell her it was my fault.

G'ma told her I was OK if w/u. U not let bad happen 2 me.

Jacques smiled at the computer screen. He wished he had a camera so they could Skype. Then he shook his head.

"That'd be pretty silly," he said to the laptop screen. "Skyping someone right across the street."

Thanks, G'ma. She's right. I watch out 4 u.

Across the street, Cienna smiled at her laptop.

"I wish he had a camera on his laptop so we could Skype," she said, looking into the lens of her webcam. Then she typed another message.

Wanna hang out 2-moro
Got 2 work @ Bean til noon. After?
4 sure. After. C u then.
C U

Jacques closed his browser and shut down his laptop. The day caught up with him in a rush. He yawned, stretched, and headed for bed.

In the few minutes it took him to fall asleep, he wondered what Scarlett was doing.

Does she even miss me? Is she lying in bed thinking about me? Or was she over me by the time she got home?

He rolled over and looked between his blinds out the window. A light was on in the Philbert's apartment and he wondered if it was Cienna's room. As he watched, the light went out. Jacques' last thoughts as he fell asleep weren't about Scarlett.

CHAPTER FIFTEEN

Four-thirty in the morning came and jolted Jacques from a cocoon of comfortable sleep he was reluctant to leave. Toby Keith was insistent in asking, "How do you like me now?"

"Stupid clock," Jacques said, slapping the snooze button to show Toby how much he didn't like him right then.

Jacques rolled over and looked out his window. All he could see through the blinds was the dim light of the street lights.

"At least it ain't raining."

He sat up and swung his legs over the side of the bed, scratched his head and then his belly before lurching to his feet and staggering to the bathroom. A short time later; showered, dressed, and slightly more awake, he stood at the door to The Bean jiggling the door handle as he turned the key. Jacques smiled when the door opened on the first try.

"Whadda ya know."

Jacques had just filled himself a Buzby Bucket when the door struck the bells and set them jangling. Knowing who it must be, Jacques turned around. "Good morning Mr. Ba -"

It wasn't Mr. Bagley with the bakery delivery. The man standing in the doorway looked familiar to Jacques, but Jacques didn't know why. For a moment, Jacques' mind tried to make the man be Scout, who had a habit of showing up early, but Scout didn't wear knit golf shirts and khaki pants with Timberland loafers. It wasn't Scout.

"Can I help you?" Jacques asked the stranger.

"I hope so. I'm looking for Jacques O'Larrity."

"What do you want with him?" Jacques asked.

His pulse quickened and his senses went on high alert. He looked around for something to use as a weapon. Keeping one hand below the counter, he used it to text his mom.

som guy just walkd in lookin for me Please be awake, Mom. Please be awake.

"Are you Jacques?" the stranger asked.

"Who are you, and why do you want to know who I am?" Jacques said, panic and anger both rising inside him.

C'mon, Mom. Please be awake.

The stranger took a step toward the counter.

"I'm not here to hurt you, son."

The stranger's head turned toward the door as Joe Bagley pushed through carrying the first tray of the morning's delivery. Joe stopped and stared.

"Hello, Joe," the stranger said. "It's been a long time."

"Sean O'Larrity," Joe said, spitting out the name like it tasted bad in his mouth. "I will be darned. Never expected to see you around here again. Hoped to never see you, anyway."

Sean's shoulders slumped and he hung his head. "I guess you've got a right to feel that way. I guess everyone does." Lifting his head, he met Joe's eyes. "But I've changed, Joe. Honestly changed my life. And I just came to see my boy."

Behind him, Jacques's Buzby Bucket made a large splash as it hit the floor by his feet, spilling hot caramel macchiato over his Top Siders and his ankles.

"Ow, oh, ouch, that's hot, ow, ow," he cried as he hopped from one foot to the other.

Joe dropped the tray of pastries he was carrying and pushed past a startled Sean to help Jacques.

"What happened, JQ? Are you all right?" Mr. Bagley asked as he rounded the counter.

Sean had moved up to the counter and was leaning over it trying to see what was wrong. Jacques stopped hopping and stagger stepped over to the ice machine.

"I spilled coffee on my feet."

Jacques opened the door to the ice machine and dumped two heaping scoops, one on each foot. Joe grabbed a hand towel from the back counter, took the scoop from Jacques, and made an ice pack from the towel.

"Go sit down and put this on them," Joe said.

"How bad is he hurt?" Sean asked.

Joe's answer was a scowl. Jacques ignored Sean, and hobbled to a table. His feet were freezing from all the ice in his shoes.

Joe pulled another towel from the counter and was just about to hand the second ice pack to Jacques when Marie burst in the door.

Marie took one look around the café and shouted, "What's going on here? Jacques, are you all right? Joe, what happened?"

She noticed Sean standing by the counter.

"Who the hell are - Sean! You can't be Sean. Sean! What are you doing here?"

Marie felt the room shift around her. If Scout hadn't walked in right behind her and caught her, she'd have hit the floor.

Scout looked at Joe.

"Trouble?"

Joe gestured at Sean with his head.

Scout glared at Sean. "You are?"

"I'm her husband," Sean said pointing at Marie, who was starting to get her focus back.

"And his father," he continued, pointing at Jacques.

"Leave now," Scout said, his voice filled with quiet menace.

"I don't think so. Who do you think you are, telling me to leave?"

"Leave now or I'll kick your…butt," Scout growled.

Joe noticed what an effort Scout made not to say what he was really thinking. Sean noticed only the steely look in Scout's eyes, yet he stood his ground.

Marie shook herself loose of Scout's hold and stood straight. She leveled a look at Sean that caused him to wilt and back away until he hit the counter.

"Why are you here, Sean?" Marie growled through clenched teeth.

Sean swallowed hard. The others were all staring at him. He licked his lips, wrung his hands, and swallowed again. Marie grew impatient with his silence.

"I'm waiting for an answer, Sean. You've been gone twelve years. Surely there must be a reason you came back. What is it?"

Jacques answered for him. "He told Mr. Bagley he came to see me."

Marie's head swiveled toward Jacques. When she saw the towels full of ice on his feet, her eyes grew wide and she rushed to his side.

"Jacques, what happened? Are you okay?"

"I spilled some coffee and some of it splashed on my feet. I'm sorry about the mess. I promise I'll clean it up."

Marie turned a hateful glare on Sean. Sean held up his hands to ward her off.

"I didn't mean for anything like that to happen, Marie. Honestly. I just wanted to see my son."

"Wasn't our reply to your message clear enough, Sean? You're not welcome here. We don't want to see you, ever again."

"I got your message, Marie."

He pushed off the counter and stood erect.

"I just couldn't be sure Jacques got mine. That's why I came. What's so bad about wanting to see my own son?"

"You want to see your son for the first time in a dozen years, so you skulk in here at five in the morning and ambush him. You oughta be ashamed of yourself."

Sean's gaze was fixed firmly on the floor. He couldn't look Marie in the eye.

"I am ashamed. I'm ashamed I ran out on you. I'm ashamed I stayed gone so long. I'm ashamed I hurt you."

He forced himself to look up and face her. She saw the tears streaming down his cheeks.

"And I'm here to apologize for all those things, to beg your forgiveness, and then I'll be gone."

Scout spoke first.

"He seeks absolution."

Everyone's head turned in his direction. Scout nodded towards Sean. "As we forgive those who trespass against us, so we are forgiven." Jacques stared at Scout, mouth agape, eyes wide in astonishment. Scout furrowed his brow.

"What?"

Jacques shook his head.

"That's the most I've ever heard you say."

"Hmm," was Scout's simple reply. Then he turned to Marie, one brow raised in question.

Marie looked from Scout to Sean and back.

"I'm supposed to just forgive him for walking out on me and Jacques and staying gone twelve years. Just like that. I'm supposed to forget everything he did and forgive him."

Scout reached out and gently touched Marie's cheek. "Forget, no. Forgive, yes."

Marie took a ragged breath. She turned to Sean, and said, "I forgave you for leaving a long time ago, Sean. I suppose I can forgive you for not coming back. You probably did us a favor.

We've done just fine without you. If my forgiveness is what you're after, fine. It's yours." She slipped her arm around Scout's waist and rested her head on his shoulder.

Sean's heart twisted in his chest, seeing Marie leaning on Scout for the strength and support he should have been the one to give. He knew he'd thrown away any chance of being that man for her long ago.

Coughing to clear his throat, Sean said, "Thank you, Marie." His attention shifted to Jacques.

"What about you, son? Can you forgive a father you've never known for not being there for you? I have no right to expect you to, but I have to ask. Please, forgive me?"

Jacques didn't know which hurt worse, the burns on his feet, or the burn in his heart.

"I don't even know you. How can I forgive you if I don't even know who you are? You're no one to me, nothing."

Jacques swallowed hard against the anger and bile rising in his throat.

Scout frowned at Jacques. Marie felt her heart breaking for her son. Joe put a comforting hand on the boy's shoulder, but kept quiet. This was Jacques' to deal with.

Sean moved to the table next to Jacques' and fell heavily into a chair.

"You have a right to hate me, son. More right than anyone. I understand you're angry with me. I offer no excuses. What I did was inexcusable, but I am truly sorry. I'm not asking for another chance. I don't deserve that. I'm just asking you to forgive me, please."

Jacques laughed, but there was no humor in it. "You think you know why I'm mad at you, mister. I'm mad at you for barging in here, messing up my morning, upsetting my mom, and annoying my friends. You keep calling me, 'son'. Cut it out. You don't deserve to call me that. You think I hate you. Ha! I don't hate you, mister. To hate you, I'd have to care, and I don't."

Jacques paused to catch his breath. Sean sat quietly and waited. Jacques narrowed his eyes at Sean.

"You want me to forgive you. Fine, you're forgiven." He gestured toward the entrance with his head. "Now there's the door. Use it one more time, but just one more time."

Jacques turned his back on Sean, head held high, mouth clamped shut. Sean stared at the back of the boy's head for several breaths, but Jacques didn't relent. With a resigned sigh, Sean rose from his chair.

"I'm staying at the Tower," he said to Marie. "I'll be in town the rest of the week." Marie nodded, but said nothing.

Sean walked around in front of Jacques, who turned his face away.

"Jacques, when you've had time to think about it, if you decide we can at least talk, I'll be at the Tower."

He handed Jacques a business card.

"My room number is on the back. Please consider giving me a chance."

Jacques didn't reach for the card, so Sean laid it on the table.

"I've got to go. My first group comes in at nine, and I've got to prepare."

No one said anything. They all just watched him as he walked to the door.

"All right, then. I'll be going. Jacques, at least think about it."

He pushed through the door and was gone. When the door bells jangled as the door closed behind him, Jacques let out a huge sigh.

"Well that sucked worse than I'd ever imagined it would."

Marie's jaw dropped. Joe looked at Jacques, stunned. Scout snorted.

Marie said, "I can't believe you said those things to him, Jacques. He is your father after all."

Jacques shook his head brusquely. "He might be Sean O'Larrity, but he doesn't get to be my father just by showing up. He'll have to prove himself first."

Joe looked at the rack of pastries on the floor. The wrapped goods were in disarray, but appeared fine otherwise.

"What do you think, Marie? Will they do?"

Joe picked up the rack and held it out to Marie.

"They look fine, Joe. Why don't you and Scout bring in the rest? With Jacques out of commission, looks like I'm gonna have to clean up that mess behind the counter."

By silent consensus, they had all decided not to talk about Sean's visit, at least until things were put in order. Customers would be showing up soon.

Jacques took the ice packs off his feet and gingerly slipped his deck shoes back on.

"I can clean that up, Mom."

"What about your feet?"

"I've had worse sunburns," Jacques replied. He winced as he took a tentative step.

"I'll be fine."

"You do know," Marie said, indicating the ice packs, "you're not supposed to use ice on burns."

"It seemed like a good idea at the time," Jacques said, forcing a smile.

Neither of them mentioned Jacques quitting the night before, or any other details of that fight.

Marie took the order pad from the hook on the wall over the decorating table and headed to the kitchen. Jacques grabbed a mop and bucket from the supply room and cleaned up the mess behind the counter. Joe and Scout brought in the rest of the bakery goods and Scout arranged them in the display case.

"Thanks Scout," Jacques said. "I appreciate you doing that."

"De nada," Scout said, helping himself to a croissant which had been crushed when Joe dropped the first tray. He held it up to show Jacques.

"For services rendered."

Jacques handed him a cup of coffee.

"Balance due."

Scout smiled and took the cup.

Marie came out from the back, put her hands on Scout's shoulders, and turned him around. Scout's eyes widened as Marie raised herself on her toes and kissed him on the cheek.

"Balance due," she said. "Thank you."

Scout stood there, coffee cup in one hand, croissant in the other, color rising in his cheeks.

"Anytime."

Joe brought in the last tray of pastries.

"That's it for today, Marie. Hope the rest of your day's less lively than the start."

"Let's hope you're right, Joe."

Jacques handed Joe his coffee. "Thanks, Mr. Bagley, for everything."

Joe took the cup and nodded to Jacques. "Glad I showed up when I did."

After Joe left, Scout said, "Hope he don't catch no grief 'bout being late."

Marie chuckled. "I don't think he'll catch any grief from the boss."

Scout took a sip of his coffee and eyed Marie suspiciously. "What's the joke?"

Marie stifled her laugh. "I'm sorry, Scout. You probably don't know. Joe owns the bakery. His son runs it for him now, since Joe retired from that part of the business. When their last delivery driver took a job with FedEx, Joe decided he'd take over the island route. Gives him a chance to visit with everyone."

Scout took a bite of his croissant, and nodded.

"Makes sense."

He glanced at the cat clock hanging behind the order counter. "Better go. Work."

Marie slipped her arms around him. "Will I see you later?"

His hands still full, Scout returned her hug with his elbows. "Yes."

Jacques, cemented in place, watched their exchange.

When Scout moved toward the door, Marie turned around and said to Jacques, "Close your mouth, JQ. You're catching flies."

Moving carefully to minimize how much his shoes rubbed against the burns on his feet, Jacques managed to get nearly everything ready before the first customer of the day walked in the door at six.

"Good morning, Jacques," Soon Lee said. "Coffee ready?"

"Mornin', Mrs. Philbert. I know how Cienna's grandma and grandpa like their coffees. What can I make for you this morning?"

Soon Lee tapped her chin while her eyes roved over the menu. "I think I'll have a hazelnut cream. Just a small one."

Jacques poured hers first, so she could sip from it while he made the other drinks. Cienna walked in as he finished mixing her grandmother's coffee.

"Hey, Mom," Cienna said as she reached the counter. "Grandma sent me over to help you carry everything." She smiled at Jacques. "Hi, JQ. You doing okay?"

Jacques winced as his shoe pinched a sensitive spot. "I'm doing all right, considering."

Cienna tilted her head. "Considering what?"

Jacques sighed and set Grandma Philbert's coffee next to Grandpa's.

"I'll tell you all about it later. I'm still trying to digest it. It's been quite a morning, for sure."

Cienna sucked her lower lip, eyes hard on Jacques. "You sure you're okay?"

Jacques managed a smile. "I'm okay. Feet just a little sore. I'll tell you all about it later."

Cienna stepped back, picked up the coffee cups, and nodded. "You can buy me lunch at Mama Leone's and spill your guts. Deal?"

Jacques laughed. "Deal."

CHAPTER SIXTEEN

Other customers came and went. Fitz Finney came in, ordered a raspberry mocha, and sat down at the bar along the wall to set up his laptop.

"Is Cameron working today?" Fitz asked.

Jacques handed him his mocha. "No. Cammy has Mondays and Tuesdays off. It's just me and Mom."

"Oh," Fitz said, his lips drooping into a pout. "Bummer."

He turned to his laptop, put on his headphones, and tuned Jacques out.

Jacques turned around in time to see Mr. Mumples walk in the door, mumbling to himself.

He brightened up when he noticed Fitz sitting at the bar.

With barely a nod to Jacques, Mr. Mumples walked over and tapped Fitz on the shoulder.

Fitz pulled off his headphones and turned around.

"Yeah, what is - oh, Mr. Mumples. Hello."

"Young man, are you still looking for a job? I find myself in need of an assistant manager, and was hoping to find you here."

A smile lit Fitz's face. "Are you serious? Sure. I'll take it."

Mr. Mumples visibly relaxed. "Fine, fine. Get packed up while I get my coffee. You can start this morning."

"You got it, sir," Fitz said, before turning and shutting down his laptop.

Mr. Mumples approached the counter. "Better make me up a Bucket sized macchiato, Jacques. I think it's going to be a busy day."

"Coming right up, Mr. Mumples. By the way, not that it's any of my business, but I think it's great, you hiring Mr. Finney."

"Needed someone right away. Kaitlynn called this morning and said she couldn't work for me anymore. No explanation. Just an apology for leaving me in the lurch. I'm just glad Fitz was still willing to come on board."

Jacques prepared Mr. Mumples' Bucket sized macchiato. "Do you need a latte for Ginger?"

Mr. Mumples frowned and shook his head. "She's taking the day off to tour the island in a surrey with Tony. He seems like a nice boy, but he's in college and she's still in high school."

He shrugged, swiped his card, and dug into his pocket for a dollar to tip Jacques.

"Thanks," Jacques said, pocketing the dollar. "Tony's a good guy, Mr. Mumples. And his dad would land on him with both feet if he stepped over the line. Ginger'll be all right."

"I'm ready when you are, Mr. Mumples," Fitz said as he walked up to the counter.

Mr. Mumples gave him a curt nod, turned, and headed for the door.

A few minutes after noon, Scout walked in.

"Hi, Scout. What are you doing here?"

"Pier, six to noon. Bean, noon to close. Mondays and Tuesdays." Scout pointed his thumb over his shoulder toward the exit.

"I'm your relief. Take off."

Jacques face twisted into a confused frown.

"Wait. What? When did this happen?"

"Yesterday. Marie and I talked. Worked it out with Mr. Kilsey. Two afternoons a week, I work here."

Marie came out from the kitchen.

"I meant to tell you this morning, JQ, but with all that went on with your…with Sean, I forgot to."

Jacques eyes flickered back and forth between Scout's face and Marie's.

"Is there something going on here you need to tell me?"

Marie and Scout exchanged a conspiratorial look. Marie said, "No, JQ. Nothing I can think of.

Scout touched his nose to hers.

"That's our story. Sticking to it."

"Oh, gross," Jacques said. "I'm outta here."

"Text me and let me know where you're at," Marie said. "Now, go on. Don't you have a date?"

"A date? No. I'm just meeting Cienna for lunch."

Seeing his mother's eyebrows raised in disbelief, Jacques said, "Uh, no. It's just two friends meeting for lunch. It is not a date."

"Whatever you say, honey," Marie said.

Nodding toward the door, she added, "Don't keep her waiting."

Jacques turned to see Cienna waiting outside on the walk. Looking back at his mom, he said, "Okay, bye."

Once outside, Cienna gave him a playful shove. "So what's the deal with Scout and your mom?"

Jacques shrugged. "I don't know. He showed up the other day before six and helped Mr. Bagley unload the truck. The next day he's working at the pier, all cleaned up, haircut and everything. This morning he showed up just as…well, let's get to Mama Leone's and I'll fill you in on this morning."

Cienna chewed her last bite of pizza while Jacques finished bringing her up to speed on the situation of his father's sudden reappearance in his life.

She wiped her mouth, crumpled up the napkin, and dropped it on her plate. "Let me see if I got this right. After twelve years of no contact at all, your father looks you up on Facebook and sends you a message. Your mom messages him back to take a hike, and then he shows up at The Bean at five in the morning, begging for forgiveness."

Jacques noisily drained the last of his diet Coke, using his hand to guide the straw around the bottom of the glass so he could get every drop, and set the glass on the table.

"Yep, that's it."

Cienna stretched her back and a small burp escaped.

"Oops, excuse me."

"I'll think about it," Jacques said, smirking.

"Well I can't take it back," Cienna quipped. Then her face grew serious. "What are you gonna do about your dad?"

Jacques picked up the last bit of his crust, gave it a good look, and dropped it on his plate.

Looking up to meet Cienna's intense gaze, he replied, "I don't know. I don't really think of him as my dad. He's been gone as long as I can remember. He might as well have been dead. For all I knew, he could have been dead."

"But he's not dead," Cienna said, leaning over the table and taking Jacques' chin in her hand. "He's back, and he's right down the street at the Coastal Tower. You've got a chance to get to know him. Or at least hear him out and decide if you want to get to know him or not."

They were sitting in a booth near the back of the dining room. Even in the early afternoon, it was dimly lit and quiet in their corner.

Jacques found he was trembling. Whether it was from the thought of confronting his dad, or the touch of Cienna's fingers on his chin, he wasn't sure.

Cienna let go of his chin and traced her fingertips along his jaw before dropping her hands to the table and sitting back. She'd felt the reaction Jacques had to the touch of her fingers on his chin.

Don't push him. He's got too much on his mind right now, she cautioned herself

"So, what are you going to do?" she asked.

Jacques waited to answer until his pulse slowed and his breathing returned to normal.

It was definitely Cienna's touch, Jacques realized. *What's going on with that?*

"Feel like taking a ride to the Tower?" he asked.

"If you want me to go with you, I will."

"Let's see if Tony's got a surrey we can ride."

He picked up the check, figured a generous tip, and left the money on the table. He shot Marie a quick text to let her know where he was going, and then waited for her reply. Jacques almost expected her to tell him not to go.

Marie replied simply, OK.

CHAPTER SEVENTEEN

On the short walk to the bike shop, Cienna and Jacques walked side-by-side, not speaking, but it was a comfortable silence. Cienna resisted the urge to reach out and take Jacques's hand.

They arrived at the bike shop and learned that Tony was still off giving Ginger her tour of the island. Tony's absence wasn't a problem as Mr. Bishop was only too happy to rent Jacques and Cienna a surrey.

"What are you two kids up to?" Mr. Bishop asked. "Gonna try and catch up with Tony and Ginger?"

"No, sir," Jacques said. "We're going down to the Tower to see someone."

"You don't say." He eyed Jacques warily. "And who might that someone be?"

The way Mr. Bishop asked made Jacques think the bike shop owner had a pretty good idea who.

"I guess you heard my father's in town," Jacques said with a nervous sigh.

"I might have heard something about that. Gotta say I'm surprised you're planning to go see him."

The way Mr. Bishop said that made it more of a question than a statement. The bike shop owner hadn't known Jacques father, having moved to the island and opened the bike shop years after Sean disappeared. But the community of year-round island residents was small and close-knit. Even though he was a relative newcomer, Mr. Bishop had heard the stories.

Jacques started to get behind the wheel of the surrey, but Cienna beat him to it and pointed at the passenger seat.

Jacques walked around the surrey to the passenger side. He turned to Mr. Bishop, who was still watching him, waiting for an answer.

"When he first came by The Bean this morning, I just wished he'd go away and stay gone." He glanced at Cienna. "But after thinking it through, I guess I should give him a chance to have his say."

"Since he's here, I guess it can't hurt," Mr. Bishop said, giving Jacques a reassuring pat on the shoulder. "Y'all drive safe. Watch out for those inlanders young lady."

"Mr. Bishop, I'm an inlander," Cienna said.

"No, you're Reggie's daughter, Herb and Bev's granddaughter. You're no inlander."

Mr. Bishop checked to be sure they both had their seat belts buckled and then gave the surrey a little push.

"Good luck, Jacques."

Traffic was steady on Sound Street, but Cienna handled the surrey like an expert. So as not to distract her, Jacques kept quiet until they were south of Eleventh Street and traffic thinned to next to nothing.

"I guess driving this thing must be like riding a bike," Jacques said. "Once you learn how, you don't forget."

"We got lots of practice last summer riding around, racing Tony, splashing through puddles on rainy days."

"Yeah," Jacques said, smiling at the memory. "That was a blast."

"JQ," Cienna said in a gentle, shy voice Jacques hadn't heard before. "I really had a good time last summer. I hated to leave. Hanging out with you was the best time I ever had."

Jacques didn't answer right away. He kept his gaze fixed out the window. Cienna chewed on her lip before going on.

"I couldn't wait to get back here when school got out."

Turning his head slightly, Jacques looked at her out of the corner of his eye. Cienna gave him a quick glance and then got her eyes back on the road.

Jacques said in a voice so soft Cienna almost missed it, "I missed you."

Cienna felt the relief flow over her like a cool breeze.

"You did?"

"Yeah."

"I missed you, too. I guess we should have stayed in touch, huh?"

"Well, we kinda did," Jacques said.

"Liking each other's' posts now and then on Facebook ain't really staying in touch, JQ."

"No, I guess not, but we'll do better this time."

"It'll be easier since I'm moving here at the end of summer and we'll be going to the same school. Duh."

"Yeah," Jacques replied, "but I'll be a sophomore and you'll just be a punk freshman."

Cienna hit the brakes and brought the surrey to a stop. She gave Jacques her best aren't-I-cute look and said, "So, you wouldn't date a freshman?"

Jacques, his pulse suddenly racing, replied, "Do you mean, you?"

Cienna released the brake and started pedaling again. In a tone somewhere between sassy and sarcastic, she said, "What do you think?"

Reaching over and putting his hand on Cienna's arm, Jacques said, "Stop the car."

"Why?" Cienna asked, making no move toward the brake.

"So I can tell you what I think," Jacques said. Then, more forcefully, "Now stop the car."

Cienna eased the surrey to the side of the road and stopped. She turned expectantly to Jacques.

"You want to know what I think?" He licked his lips and took the leap. "I think if I'd known, if I'd had any idea, that you thought of me like that, I'd have never given Scarlett a second look. Why didn't you give me a clue, toss me a hint, something?"

Cienna leaned away from him in her seat. "I didn't say anything because you never acted like you wanted to be anything but friends. Until I got back here and saw you again, I wasn't even sure about how I felt. The minute I saw you, I knew I didn't want to be just friends, but before I could give you a hint, you were with Scarlett. Now I don't know how to feel. I don't want to be your rebound."

A lightness filled Jacques heart, and the smile forming on his lips was matched by a brightness in his eyes Cienna'd only seen once since she came back to the island, the day at the theater, at the end of the movie when he'd looked at her just before his phone rang.

Jacques reached out and pressed his hand to her cheek.

"You'd never be a rebound, Cienna."

She leaned into his palm, relishing the feel of its warmth against her face.

"I'd better not be, JQ."

Jacques slid his hand behind her head, pulling her toward him as he leaned toward her. His heart was pounding in his chest.

Cienna licked her lips as Jacques closed the distance between them. Then his lips were on hers. Gently, but insistently. Her mouth opened slightly, and his tongue had just reached out to touch her lips when her elbow hit the brake release and the surrey started rolling.

"Oh crap," Cienna said, grabbing for the brake.

Jacques sat up so quickly he almost rolled out the other side of the surrey. He might have if his seatbelt hadn't been buckled.

"Good thing Mr. Bishop made us put our seat belts on before letting us go."

Cienna got them stopped, but the moment had passed.

"I guess we ought to get on down to the Tower," she said, breathing hard, and not just from the momentary panic of having the brake let go.

Jacques righted himself in the passenger seat. "Yeah, I guess we should." He looked over at Cienna.

"You okay?"

Her smile washed over him like a warm rain.

"I'm great."

The pleasant feeling Jacques was basking in after the kiss left him as they got closer to the Coastal Tower Resort. By the time they rolled through the gate and parked the surrey near the entrance, he was practically vibrating with tension.

Cienna laid a hand on his arm, leaned across the seat, and kissed Jacques' cheek.

"It's going to be fine. I'll go in with you, if you want."

Jacques swallowed several times against the dryness in his throat. "Thanks, but this is something I need to do by myself." He turned pleading eyes on her.

"You'll wait for me though, won't you?"

"I'll be right here."

Jacques took a deep breath, climbed out of the surrey, and headed for the door. Cienna watched until he disappeared through the revolving door, and then sat back to wait.

The lobby of the Coastal Tower Resort was designed to impress. It was a soaring four-story atrium of marble, glass, and stainless steel, softened by islands of live plants strategically placed to channel guests toward the different wings of the resort, depending on whether they were seeking dining, drinking, dancing, or to satisfy other desires.

Jacques stepped from the revolving door, scanned the lobby, and was about to walk over to the registration desk when the uniformed bell captain, an acne scarred twenty-something that Jacques assumed was a UNCW student working a summer job so he could stay at the beach, approached him.

"Can I help you, young man?"

Jacques cleared his throat, showed him the card with Sean's room number on the back, and said, "I'm here to see Mr. O'Larrity."

The bell captain looked at the card and motioned for Jacques to follow him to the concierge desk.

There, he handed Sean's card to the concierge. "This young man is here to see Mr. O'Larrity."

The concierge looked at Jacques, taking in Jacques' blue Parisian Bean t-shirt, khaki cargo shorts, and well-worn deck shoes.

"I'll ring his room and see if he's available," the concierge, an attractive woman who wore her light brown hair pulled back in a severe bun said,

"Who should I say is here to see him?"

Jacques squared his shoulders and returned her condescending look with what he hoped was a confident glare.

“Tell him it’s his son. My name is Jacques O’Larrity.”

CHAPTER EIGHTEEN

The concierge's stiff expression relaxed and she smiled at Jacques before picking up the house phone.

After a short wait, she said into the phone, "Mr. O'Larrity, this is Jessica at the concierge desk. A young man, Jacques O'Larrity, is here to see you. Should I send him up?"

Jessica looked at Jacques, but her eyes were unfocused as she listened to Sean on the phone.

"Yes, sir. I'll ask him to wait for you."

"Mr. O'Larrity asked that you wait for him here. You may have a seat over there."

Jessica pointed to a pair of leather covered armchairs flanking a small, round, end-table by the nearest raised island of live trees and ferns.

Jacques sank into the padded chair. He didn't have to wait long. Rising as Sean walked up, Jacques decided to address his estranged father with polite courtesy and held out his hand. “Hello, sir. I hope I didn’t interrupt you or anything.”

Sean stopped, looked at Jacques’ outstretched hand for an awkward moment, obviously hoping for more, and then gripped it in a firm handshake.

“No, not at all. I was just going over a few notes for this afternoon’s talk. I’m glad you came.” Sean gestured toward the tables near the juice bar in the atrium. “Let’s get something to drink, and then we can talk.”

Jacques, familiar with the tales of his father’s drinking, raised his brow.

Sean read Jacques’ expression. “It’s a juice bar, Jacques. No booze. I know what you’ve probably heard about me, but I’ve been sober for four years now. I got help, and now I help others like me.”

“Others like you?” Jacques echoed in question as they walked down the short flight of stairs into the atrium.

“Alcoholics who’ve lost everything,” Sean said. “Jobs, homes, families.” He paused for a long moment.

“Self-respect. People who’d do anything for their next drink. And I give talks like the one this afternoon to health care professionals who work with those people. I give them a first person account of what it’s like to live like that.”

Jacques heard the regret and self-recrimination in Sean’s voice. He looked at his father. Sean’s eyes were moist. He blinked to clear them.

“C’mon,” Sean said, pointing at the juice bar. “They make a great strawberry-banana smoothie.”

"What can I get for you gents today?" the cocoa skinned girl behind the juice bar asked in a Jamaican accent as Jacques and Sean sidled up.

Jacques stifled a laugh. He knew the girl, whose name tag identified her as Bryah, had graduated from South Hanover that year. As far as Jacques knew, Bryah had never been to Jamaica.

"Two strawberry-banana smoothies please, Bryah," Sean said. "I told my son, Jacques here, that you make the best."

He turned to Jacques, and added, "Must be she uses some of that Caribbean magic."

"Must be," Jacques said, biting his lip to keep from laughing.

Sean wondered what Jacques found so funny. He turned back to Bryah and noticed she was trying not to laugh, too.

"Why do I get the feeling you two heard a joke I missed?"

Jacques looked around to see if anyone else could hear, and then, in a quiet voice, told his father, "Bryah just graduated from South Hanover, Dad. She was valedictorian. Born and raised right over the bridge in Myrtle Grove."

Sean looked at Bryah, who nodded. "Don't tell the tourists, please. Dey tip better if dey tink I'm from de islands, mon."

Sean joined their laughter. "Your secret's safe with me."

Then suddenly, he stopped. A stunned expression replaced the laughter on his face.

"Jacques, you called me "Dad."

Jacques stopped laughing, too. His brow furrowed as he played back his last few words in his head. A tentative smile twitched at his lips.

"I guess I did. Is that okay?"

"Okay?" Sean said. "Yeah, it's okay. It's very okay."

Bryah handed them their smoothies and they moved to a table.

"If we're gonna be here long," Jacques said, "I've got a friend waiting outside. Is it all right if I ask her to come in?"

"Her, huh?" Sean said. "Sure, ask her to join us." He pressed his lips into a thin line and his eyes nearly closed. "There's someone I want you to meet too, but first there's something I need to tell you."

Jacques looked up from his phone, where he'd just texted Cienna and asked her to come in.

His tone was guarded as he asked, "What do you need to tell me?"

Sean fidgeted in his chair, took a sip of his smoothie, and rubbed his jaw. "Seeing you was the most important reason I came back, Jacques, but it's not the only reason."

Sean seemed to be taking a moment to frame his next words. Jacques took a sip of his smoothie - it was as good as Sean said it would be - and waited.

"Did you know your mother had divorce papers drawn up years ago, but she never filed them?" Sean asked.

Jacques shook his head. His mother had never said anything to him about it.

"Evidently, she didn't want it to wind up in court, and she thought that's what I'd do if she filed them without my signing off on the split. Back then I probably would have, too." Sean gave Jacques a moment to digest that bit of news.

Jacques tilted his head back and looked up toward the glass roof of the atrium, soaring four stories above.

When he lowered his head, he looked at Sean. "And now?"

"Now," Sean said, "Now I'm ready to sign the papers. I'm not going to ask anything of Marie. I'll sign with no conditions, no claims. Just one request."

"What's that?" Jacques asked through a tight throat.

"I want us to keep in touch. I'd like to be able to visit you now and then, and maybe have you come visit me in Chapel Hill."

Jacques took a ragged breath and let it out slowly. He was saved from having to respond by Cienna's arrival.

"Hi JQ," Cienna said.

She turned to Sean. "You must be Mr. O'Larrity. How do you do? I'm Cienna Philbert."

Sean took her hand and shook it gently.

"Philbert? You're not Reggie Philbert's daughter are you?"

Cienna blushed. "Yes, that's me. Reggie's little girl."

Sean sat back and smiled. "Imagine, Reggie Philbert having a daughter so grown up and beautiful."

Cienna's blush deepened.

"Thank you, sir."

"My dad lives in Chapel Hill," Jacques blurted out, not knowing what else to say.

"Is that so?" Cienna said, pulling out a chair and sitting down.

Bryah walked over to the table. "Would da little lady like some'ting to drink?"

Sean said, "Go ahead, Cienna. It's on me."

"I'll have whatever you guys are drinking," Cienna said, pointing to Jacques glass.

"Anoder strawberry-banana smoodie comin' right up," Bryah said, with a wink at Sean.

Sean winked at Jacques, and said to Cienna, "Bryah sounds like she came straight from the Caribbean, doesn't she?"

Cienna shrugged. "She's pretty good with accents. Last year she worked at the Lonely Pirate and did a really good pirate brogue."

Sean chuckled and shook his head. "I guess I'm the only one who thought she was a real Rastafarian girl."

When Bryah brought Cienna her smoothie, she set it down with an, "Arrgh, you saw through my disguise, missy. Don't go given me away now."

She patted Cienna's shoulder and, with a satisfied smile on her face, returned to the juice bar.

Sean waited until Cienna tried her smoothie before turning the conversation back to his purpose for visiting the island.

"I mentioned before Jacques, that there's someone I want you to meet."

Sean turned and waved to a lady sitting alone at a table on the other side of the atrium.

She waved back, stood, and walked over to their table.

When the lady he'd signaled got close, Sean stood and put his arm around her waist.

"Jacques, Cienna, this is Lincy Sanders. Lincy, this is my son Jacques and his friend Cienna."

"It's a pleasure to meet you both," Lincy said.

Jacques stared speechless at Lincy. From the way Sean's arm possessively encircled her waist, they were more than friends. The top of Lincy's head reached just past Sean's shoulder. Her auburn hair was cut short, in an almost masculine style. Her loose fitting clothing hid her figure, but she moved with the confidence and grace of an athlete or dancer.

"Jacques, Sean told me he had a teenage son, but I wasn't expecting you to be so tall, or handsome. You must get your good looks from your mother."

Jacques wanted to be offended that this woman would even mention his mother, but something about the open and friendly way she said it, kept it from bothering him.

Cienna delivered an elbow to his ribs, breaking him out of his trance.

"Uh, thank you. It's nice to meet you, too."

"Why don't we all sit down," Sean said, holding out a seat for Lincy.

Without waiting to ask, Bryah prepared and brought Lincy a raspberry-kiwi smoothie.

"Thanks, Bryah. Didn't even have to ask, did you?"

"I remember what you like Miss Lincy," Bryah said, not bothering with any accent. "Y'all enjoy."

Jacques sipped on his smoothie. He had no idea what to say to Lincy or his dad. Cienna didn't have that problem.

"So Lincy, how did you and Jacques's dad meet?"

Lincy looked at Sean. He put his hand on hers, and nodded once. Lincy took a deep breath.

"We met four years ago in rehab. Sean and I were in the same group. As we went through the classes and the sessions, we became friends. At the end of the twelve weeks, we graduated, and our sentences were commuted. After that, we stayed in touch, attending meetings together and acting as each other's support network. Our friendship grew into love and now, well, it's pretty obvious, isn't it?"

Jacques was staring hard at his father. "Your sentences?"

Sean looked down at his hands. "About five years ago, I got my third DUI in less than a year. My license had already been suspended. The judge gave me a choice. check myself into the rehab program to dry out, or ninety days in jail."

Lincy took his hand in hers and squeezed. "My story is pretty much the same."

No one said anything for several long minutes. Sean finally broke the silence. "So Jacques, that guy at the coffee shop this morning. How long have he and Marie been together?"

"You mean Scout," Jacques said. "That's actually a very recent thing. I don't know that she'd like me talking about it."

Not that I'd have any idea what to tell you, anyway, Jacques thought to himself. *I don't know any more about Mom and Scout than you do.*

"Okay, then. I won't pry."

Sean's phone beeped. He pulled it out of his pocket and checked the screen. After he showed it to Lincy he said, "Time to get ready for my next presentation."

To Jacques he said, "Sorry son, but I have to go. This is my last session for today. Lincy and I are leaving tomorrow morning, so I was hoping, maybe we could meet somewhere for dinner or something."

"It's all-you-can-eat taco night at Los Amigos," Jacques said. "Mom and I usually go."

Cienna kicked him under the table.

"Ouch. I mean, oh, maybe that's not a good idea."

Sean said, "Actually, that would be fine. I'll call Marie after my session and let her know I need to talk to her. I just hope she'll listen."

"I could give her a heads up," Jacques said. "Let her know why you want to meet."

Sean shook his head. "No, that's okay. I'd rather she hear it from me."

Jacques nodded. "Yeah, that'd probably be better."

"I'll see you there then," Sean said. "Cienna, will you be coming, too?"

Cienna looked at Jacques, who inclined his head and raised his brow in a hopeful gesture. "If it's okay with my folks, I'll will." She looked at Lincy. "Are you coming?"

Lincy licked her lips. "I think it might be a good idea for me to sit this one out."

Sean's phone beeped again. He stood. "I hate this, but I really have to go, Jacques. I'll see you at Los Amigos?"

Jacques rose from his seat. "Okay. I'll see you there."

After saying again how pleased she was to meet them, Lincy left with Sean. Jacques sat back down with Cienna.

"We might as well finish our smoothies," he said, raising his glass in a mock salute.

Cienna clinked her glass against his. "Here's to interesting afternoons, and an even more interesting evening to come."

CHAPTER NINETEEN

The Parisian Bean had closed for the day by the time Jacques and Cienna returned from meeting Sean at the Tower. Cienna went to The News Stand to ask her parents if she could go to dinner with Jacques and his mom at Los Amigos. Jacques went up to the apartment to find Marie.

"Hi JQ," Marie said when he walked in. She had papers and receipts spread over the kitchen table. "How'd things go with your father?"

Jacques sat down across the table from her. "Pretty good. Better than I expected. He said he was going to call you. Did he?"

"Oh, yes. He called," Marie said, putting down her pencil and taking a sip from her coffee mug. "He's meeting us at Los Amigos for dinner. Said he had something he needed to talk to me about."

"He mentioned something about coming to dinner," Jacques said. "Oh, and Cienna might come, too. I hope that's okay. My...father kind of invited her."

Marie set her mug down and examined Jacques closely. "He did, huh? Interesting. Is he under the impression you two are a couple?"

"No, I don't think so. We told him we were just friends."

Jacques wondered whether he should mention Lincy, or that his dad asked about Scout.

"Did you tell him anything about Scarlett?" Marie asked.

"There wasn't anything to tell. We hung out for a few days, and then she was gone. I'll never see her again. End of story."

Jacques wished he was as over the episode as he tried to make it sound.

"I see," Marie said. "Do you know if Sean's bringing his girlfriend with him tonight?" She tried to sound nonchalant, but Jacques could hear the tension in her voice.

"You know about Lincy?" he asked.

"Is that her name?" Marie said. "I didn't know her name, but Shelia, the events manager at the Tower, told me she'd seen Sean with a lady friend. I guess they're there doing some sort of presentation to a group of counselors or something. I delivered a cake for their luncheon today. So you met her?"

"Yes, ma'am," Jacques said. "She was there."

Marie nodded. "What did you think of her?"

Jacques shrugged. "She was okay. Nice enough I suppose."

"Is she going to be there tonight?"

"I don't think so," Jacques said. "Did you ask Scout to come?"

Marie dropped the pencil she'd been twirling in her fingers. "Why would I ask Scott, er, Scout to come?"

Jacques cocked his head and squinted at Marie. "Who's Scott?"

Marie sighed, and smiled. "Scott is Scout's real name. Scott Yardray. And yes, I asked him to join us for tacos tonight, before I knew your father was coming."

"Are you and Scout, you know, is he your boyfriend now?" Jacques asked.

The idea of his mom with a boyfriend gave him a funny feeling, like a chill blowing over him.

"I don't know if I'd call him my boyfriend, yet," Marie said, grinning at the expression on Jacques' face. "But you never know."

Jacques swallowed against the queasy feeling the idea of his mom with a boyfriend gave him.

"So, Scout's coming tonight. Does my father know that?"

"No," Marie said.

"No, my dad doesn't know?" Jacques asked.

Marie's brows arched when Jacques called Sean his "dad," but she let it go.

"No, Scout's not coming," she said. "We're taking things one step at a time, and going to dinner with you and me is a step he's not quite ready to take."

As it turned out, all the Philberts went to Los Amigos for all-you-can-eat taco night. The six of them sat together at a table near the front. Jacques, Marie, and Sean sat at a table in a quieter corner near the back of the overflow dining room. Los Amigos always filled the overflow dining room on taco night during the summer.

Conversation between Marie and Sean was strained at first. Jacques felt like he was sitting on a pin cushion with all the pins pointy end out. Once they'd ordered and their drinks arrived, but before the first batch of tacos was delivered, Sean told Marie he was ready to grant her the divorce she'd asked for those twelve years ago, just before he'd disappeared from their lives.

Marie took the news stoically. She shed no tears, made no recriminations. She simply thanked Sean for letting her know. After that, they all relaxed, and while Jacques wouldn't have said they had a good time, it wasn't unpleasant either.

When they'd eaten their fill of tacos, Sean insisted on picking up the check. Marie insisted they split the bill, but not too fiercely. In the end, she graciously agreed to let Sean take care of it.

Jacques walked with Sean to the cashier's stand. Marie stopped to talk to the Philbert's. After he'd paid, Sean asked Jacques to step outside with him before Marie came out.

"Jacques," Sean said, holding his hands clasped before him as if in prayer. "I wish I didn't have to leave in the morning. As soon as I can, I'll come back and stay for a while, if you want me to."

"I'm not sure my mom would be crazy about the idea, but yeah, I think I'd be okay that."

Sean smiled. "And maybe we can keep in touch on Facebook, you know. I'll let you know where I'm at and you can tell me what's new with you."

Jacques nodded. "We could do that."

"Good, good," Sean said.

His phone buzzed and after he checked it he looked at Jacques, and said, "I really have to go. I'll miss you, son. You take care."

"You, too, ...Dad," Jacques said, offering his hand for a handshake.

Sean took the offered hand, and then pulled Jacques to him for a manly hug; hands clasped in front, fist pounds on the back. Jacques stiffened at first, but forced himself to relax and give Sean a couple of fist pounds of his own.

There were several seconds of awkward silence following the hug before Sean nodded to Jacques and walked to his rented Sonata. Jacques stood on the sidewalk in front of Los Amigos and watched his father drive off. He turned to go back inside and almost ran over Cienna.

"How long have you been standing there?" Jacques asked, after he recovered his balance.

"I walked out just as your dad drove off," Cienna said. "So, how'd it go?"

Jacques glanced down the road where his father'd just driven off, and said, "Okay, I guess. He and my mom agreed about the divorce and stuff. He says he'll come back as soon as he can."

Jacques stuck his hands in his pockets, looked at the sidewalk, and scuffed his shoe against the curb.

"I'll believe it when he walks in the door of The Bean again."

"I think he will," Cienna said.

She put her arm through Jacques' and steered down the road toward the beach.

"He wants to make up for lost time, to get to know you."

Jacques shrugged and walked along with her down Seventh Street.

When they walked past the theater, he asked, "Where are we going, anyway?"

Cienna laid her head against his shoulder. "I told your mom and my folks that we wanted to take a walk down by the pier after supper. They said to just make sure we're home by ten."

"You told them that, huh?" Jacques said. "And what are we going to do down by the pier?"

"You're a smart guy," Cienna said, squeezing his arm. "I'm sure you'll think of something."

CHAPTER TWENTY

Over the next week and a half, Cienna met Jacques at The Bean every day at noon when he got off work. They spent sunny days riding bikes, hanging out at the beach, playing putt-putt, or fishing on the pier.

On those rare days it rained, they'd take in a movie, play at the arcade, or just hang around The News Stand reading. A couple of times they double-dated with Tony and Ginger; once to hear a band play at Greenleaf Park, once to see a Hammerheads game at Legion Stadium.

They'd shared more kisses, but none had the intensity of the kiss they'd shared in the surrey on the way to the Towers. The night they walked down by the pier, the day of The Kiss, they agreed it wasn't the right time for them to get too serious.

And then it was time for Cienna to go home.

"I can't believe you've got to leave in the morning," Jacques said.

They were sitting on the pier watching the moonlight shimmering on the water. Jacques was holding Cienna's hand.

Cienna squeezed his hand, and said, "I know. But I'll be back at the end of August. And then I won't ever have to leave again."

Jacques turned, his other hand coming up and cradling her chin, turning her face towards his.

"That's over two months away. Why can't you stay here with your grandparents? It's not like you have to get back to school or anything."

Cienna's sad smile hurt Jacques deep inside.

"I need to help my mom get ready for the move. I want to say good-bye to my friends. It won't be that long, Jacques. You'll see. You'll be so busy you probably won't even miss me."

"Only every morning when you don't come to get your grandpa's coffee. And every lunch time when I get off work and you won't be there waiting for me. And every day when I look across the street and know you're not there. I'll only miss you those times."

Cienna jumped off the bench. "Hey, it's my last night on the island until the end of summer. I don't want to spend it moping around. Bet I can beat you at putt-putt."

Jacques stretched, and looked up at her through narrowed eyes. "As if." They played putt-putt, and she won.

"Did you let me win?" Cienna asked him when they sat down in the snack bar with sodas and a bag of popcorn.

Jacques popped a piece of popcorn into his mouth and chewed it slowly before answering her question.

"Who, me? I'd never do such a thing."

Cienna threw a piece of popcorn at him and it bounced off his forehead.

"Yeah, right."

Pointing to the entrance to the Go-Kart track, Jacques said, "Bet you can't keep up with me for four laps."

Cienna finished off the last of her diet Coke and said, "You're on."

Four laps later, she conceded defeat, sort of.

"You wouldn't have beaten me if that kid in the red car hadn't cut me off. I was gaining on you."

Jacques laughed. "How'd he get past you if you were gaining on me?"

Cienna punched him playfully on the arm. "He got past you, too. His car was way faster than ours."

"For a fact," Jacques said. "What do you want to do now?"

Cienna pulled out her phone and scowled when she checked the time.

"It's almost ten. I gotta get home. We've got to be up at 'O-Dark-Thirty,' as my dad says, to make our flight out of ILM."

Jacques didn't want the night to end. The next day Cienna was leaving, and it would be two endless months, the whole rest of summer, until she came back.

At least when she comes back, she's coming back to stay.

They walked back to The News Stand hand in hand. At the bottom of the stairs leading up to the Philbert's apartment, they stopped and faced each other.

"Will I see you in the morning before you go?" Jacques asked.

"My dad says we have to leave by five. You know, because our flight's at seven and there's all those security checks and stuff."

"Yeah," Jacques said. "That's early. But I'm down to open up the shop at five a.m. If I come down a little early, I can have you guys come coffee made to take on the ride."

"It's not that long of a ride from here to the airport, Jacques, but thanks," Cienna said.

The door at the top of the stairs opened and Cienna's mother called out, "Cienna, is that you down there? You need to come on up, dear. We've got an early morning tomorrow. Tell Jacques good-night. You'll see him again soon."

"I'll be right up, Mom," Cienna called up the stairs. Her mother didn't answer, but they heard the door close.

Cienna said, "I better go on up."

"I know," Jacques said.

Instead of moving toward the stairs, Cienna threw her arms around Jacques. Her move caught him by surprise, but he quickly recovered and put his arms around her. She burrowed her face in his shoulder and he could feel her sobbing.

"Hey, hey," he said. "It's going to be all right. It's just a couple of months."

Cienna turned her face up so she could look into his eyes. "I'm gonna miss you so much."

Jacques reached up and ran his hand over her hair. "I'm gonna miss you, too."

He lowered his head until their lips met. There was nothing tentative about their kiss. Jacques pressed hard against her mouth, his lips parting, his tongue darting out to caress Cienna's lips and convince them to part for him.

Her lips did, and their tongues danced, twisting and curling around each other, tasting of each other. Cienna's hand slipped behind Jacques' head, pulling him down so they could deepen the kiss. He pulled her tight against him, not wanting to let her go, not wanting this moment to end.

Cienna felt her knees grow weak. She began to sag against Jacques, breaking off the kiss.

He held her up and she laid her head on his chest.

Slowly, she straightened up and moved away from Jacques, towards the stairs. Jacques started to move toward her, but Cienna held up her hand to stop him.

"No, Jacques," Cienna said, her breath coming in gasps. "You can't come with me right now."

Jacques stopped. Every fiber of his being wanted to take her in his arms again and not let her go. But he knew she had to go. For a time, he had to let her go.

Cienna blinked back tears.

"I hope you still feel this way about me when I come back. You won't go finding another girl while I'm gone, will you Jacques?"

Jacques fought back his own tears. "There couldn't be another girl who could make me feel like you do, Cienna. I...."

"Don't say it, Jacques. Wait and tell me when I come back."

She ran to the top of the stairs. Standing at the door, she turned to look down at him.

"You'll wait for me, won't you?"

Jacques smiled up at her through his tears.

"I'll be right here."

ABOUT THE AUTHOR

DW Davis is an independent author of young adult romance novels usually told from the guy's perspective. DW's writing reflects his memories of growing up along the North Carolina coast near Wrightsville and Carolina Beaches. DW left that area when he graduated high school, and traveled half-way around the world and back collecting memories and experiences which help shape his characters. Now back in eastern North Carolina, DW enjoys bringing to life characters whose adventures take place in his favorite part of the world.

.Special Note From The Author

I hope you found as much enjoyment reading The Boy From Buzby Beach as I did writing it. If so, please consider leaving a review on Amazon.

I love connecting with my readers and would enjoy hearing from you. Here are some quick links on the next page to follow and stay connected.

DW Davis

CONNECT WITH DW DAVIS

FB Author Page -

https://www.facebook.com/RiverSailorLiterary

Twitter Link -

https://twitter.com/DWDavisRSL

Google+ -

https://plus.google.com/+DWDavis/posts

Amazon Author Page –

http://www.amazon.com/author/dwdavis

On About.me –

http://about.me/dwdavis

On Pinterest -

http://www.pinterest.com/dwdavisrsl/

River Sailor Literary Web Page –

http://www.riversailorliterary.com/

Made in the USA
Columbia, SC
15 July 2018